THE CENTRAL
INTELLIGENCE

Borgo Press Books by JOHN RUSSELL FEARN

1,000-Year Voyage: A Science Fiction Novel * *Anjani the Mighty: A Lost Race Novel* (Anjani #2) * *Black Maria, M.A.: A Classic Crime Novel* (Black Maria #1) * *A Case for Brutus Lloyd* * *The Crimson Rambler: A Crime Novel* * *Death in Silhouette* (Black Maria #5) * *Don't Touch Me: A Crime Novel* * *Dynasty of the Small: Classic Science Fiction Stories* * *The Empty Coffins: A Mystery of Horror* * *The Fourth Door: A Mystery Novel* * *From Afar: A Science Fiction Mystery* * *Fugitive of Time: A Classic Science Fiction Novel* * *The G-Bomb: A Science Fiction Novel* * *The Genial Dinosaur* (Herbert the Dinosaur #2) * *The Gold of Akada: A Jungle Adventure Novel* (Anjani #1) * *Here and Now: A Science Fiction Novel* * *Into the Unknown: A Science Fiction Tale* * *Last Conflict: Classic Science Fiction Stories* * *Legacy from Sirius: A Classic Science Fiction Novel* * *The Man from Hell: Classic Science Fiction Stories* * *The Man Who Was Not: A Crime Novel* * *Manton's World: A Classic Science Fiction Novel* * *Moon Magic: A Novel of Romance* (as Elizabeth Rutland) * *The Murdered Schoolgirl: A Classic Crime Novel* (Black Maria #2) * *One Remained Seated: A Classic Crime Novel* (Black Maria #3) * *One Way Out: A Crime Novel* (with Philip Harbottle) * *Pattern of Murder: A Classic Crime Novel* * *Reflected Glory: A Dr. Castle Classic Crime Novel* * *Robbery Without Violence: Two Science Fiction Crime Stories* * *Rule of the Brains: Classic Science Fiction Stories* * *Shattering Glass: A Crime Novel* * *The Silvered Cage: A Scientific Murder Mystery* * *Slaves of Ijax: A Science Fiction Novel* * *Something from Mercury: Classic Science Fiction Stories* * *The Space Warp: A Science Fiction Novel* * *A Thing of the Past* (Herbert the Dinosaur #1) * *Thy Arm Alone: A Classic Crime Novel* (Black Maria #4) * *The Time Trap: A Science Fiction Novel* * *Vision Sinister: A Scientific Detective Thriller* * *Voice of the Conqueror: A Classic Science Fiction Novel* * *What Happened to Hammond? A Scientific Mystery* * *Within That Room!: A Classic Crime Novel* * *World Without Chance*

THE GOLDEN AMAZON SAGA

1. *World Beneath Ice* * 2. *Lord of Atlantis* * 3. *Triangle of Power* * 4. *The Amethyst City* * 5. *Daughter of the Amazon* * 6. *Quorne Returns* * 7. *The Central Intelligence* * 8. *The Cosmic Crusaders* * 9. *Parasite Planet* * 10. *World Out of Step* * 11. *The Shadow People* * 12. *Kingpin Planet* * 13. *World in Reverse* * 14. *Dwellers in Darkness* * 15. *World in Duplicate* * 16. *Lords of Creation* * 17. *Duel with Colossus* * 18. *Standstill Planet* * 19. *Ghost World* * 20. *Earth Divided* * 21. *Chameleon Planet* (with Philip Harbottle)

THE CENTRAL INTELLIGENCE

THE GOLDEN AMAZON SAGA, BOOK SEVEN

JOHN RUSSELL FEARN

Edited by Philip Harbottle

THE BORGO PRESS
MMXIII

THE CENTRAL INTELLIGENCE

FIRST BORGO PRESS EDITION

Published by Wildside Press LLC

www.wildsidebooks.com

DEDICATION

To the memory of Mrs. Jeanne D. James

CONTENTS

THE GOLDEN AMAZON
by Philip Harbottle

In 1943 British writer John Russell Fearn decided to quit writing for the American pulp science fiction magazines, and to concentrate instead on books for the English market. Within a very few years he became established as a leading novelist in several genres, not only science fiction, but also mystery and detective fiction, and westerns.

His first new SF novel, *The Golden Amazon*, was published by World's Work in April 1944. In this story, a little girl of three years of age is made the subject of an idealistic scientist's illegal glandular experiments. The scientist's dream is to end world wars by creating a woman devoid of the usual lusts and frailties of mankind, who upon reaching maturity would institute a benign scientific rule. But the apparently successful experiment has a flaw: it instills into the girl a hatred for all men, and a ruthless cruelty. Her supernatural scientific gifts enable her to master atomic power, and practically leads her to destroy the world. She breaks the will and strength of men, and elevates women to positions of wealth and power. She also discovers human synthesis, and by this means she is able to escape retribution when she is eventually overthrown. She is seen to collapse and die, a victim of consuming ketabolism, echoing the memorable finale of Rider Haggard's *She*. In actuality, it was only her synthetic image, and this paved the way for the *Golden Amazon Returns*, and further sequels

Fearn sold reprint rights in the first novel to the prestigious Canadian magazine, the Toronto *Star Weekly*. The magazine carried a special Comics Supplement, the centre section of which was a 'complete novel', published in newspaper format. Aimed at a general readership, the novels were written by the top popular novelists of the day, including John Dickson Carr, Ellery Queen, and P. G. Wodehouse. They sold hundreds of thousands of copies, and the novels were syndicated to several American newspapers in the Maine and New York areas. The Amazon novels enjoyed extraordinary popularity (especially with Canadian housewives), and ran for the next sixteen years following the appearance of the first novel in the March 3, 1945 issue, ending with Fearn's sudden death in September 1960, aged only fifty-two. His final two Amazon novels appeared posthumously.

During Fearn's lifetime, only the first six novels were published in British hardcover editions from the World's Work in England, after appearing in the *Star Weekly*. This was because the publishers discontinued their entire fiction line in 1954. However, the Amazon novels continued to appear in the *Star Weekly*, eventually notching up twenty-four titles.

Fearn had resold paperback rights to the Canadian publisher Harlequin Books, but after publishing only the first three titles, they stopped publishing SF and other genre fiction to concentrate on their famous Romances line.

Meanwhile, as early as 1949, Fearn had realized that the Amazon series had the potential to run indefinitely. This presented him with a problem, however. The 'origin story' of the Golden Amazon was conceived and actually set during the Second World War. Subsequent novels were written during the war and the immediate postwar period, and projected their stories only a few decades into the future.

He very astutely realized that to keep ahead of reality, he needed to move the Amazon *further* into the future—first into the outer solar system, and thence to the stars. So with the seventh novel, he introduced a new main character, Abna of Atlantis—someone as equally intelligent, and even stronger than herself. These dynamics provided him with an *interstellar* canvas, thus ensuring that the series would remain ahead of reality.

Fearn's strategy was a great success, and the Amazon novels retained their popularity, ending only with his tragically early death in 1960. By then he had written a further twenty Amazon novels, and made preliminary notes for his next (which would later be written by Fearn's biographer, Philip Harbottle).

Long after Fearn's death, his entire Amazon series

would eventually see print from the pioneering US small press Gryphon Books in limited paperback editions, and later by the Canadian Battered Silicon Dispatch Box small press in their hardcover Omnibus series.

This new Borgo Press paperback series will be the first trade edition of all twenty-one of these later novels by Fearn, beginning with the seventh novel in the original series. First published in 1949 as *Conquest of the Amazon*, I have edited it slightly as *World Beneath Ice* (The Golden Amazon Saga, Book One) so that it can be read and enjoyed by new readers who may be totally unfamiliar with what had gone before. Subsequent novels have also been slightly edited for modern readers.

The publishers hope that this new series may create many more "fans of the Amazon." Meanwhile, any reader interested in seeking out the earlier six Golden Amazon novels will find that they are readily available on the internet, and in numerous earlier paperback and hardcover editions.

* * * * * * * * * *

To date, readers can enjoy the following new Borgo Press editions:

Book One: *World Beneath Ice*

In destroying the threat of an alien invasion, the Golden Amazon had inadvertently caused a decline in the sun's heat, encasing Earth in an ice sheet that threatens to eliminate humanity. The Amazon encounters Abna, a descendant of Atlantis, stronger and even more scientifically advanced than she, and the ruler of an Atlantean colony still surviving in a protected environment on Jupiter. She refuses his offer of marriage, but agrees to form an alliance in order to restore the sun and save the Earth. One thing that Abna has not told the Amazon is that all the females of his race have been wiped out by a bacilli infection....

Book Two: *Lord of Atlantis*

A gigantic ridge of land rises from the Atlantic floor, causing massive tidal waves on either side of the ocean. Even stranger, both England and America are then assailed by an invasion of prehistoric monsters! A gigantic domed city rests on the newly risen plateau, whilst out in space an alien spacecraft orbits the Earth. Such are the mysteries and challenges facing the Golden Amazon, self-appointed governess of Earth, as she struggles to unravel the maze of mystery that was the deadly legacy of Atlantis!

Book Three: *Triangle of Power*

The marriage of Violet Ray Brant—better known as The Golden Amazon—and Abna of Atlantis should have ushered in an era of peace and scientific prosperity to the people of Earth. But an unexpected turn of events finds Abna betrayed and marooned on a satellite of Jupiter, and the Amazon flung far beyond the Solar System. With Earth's two protectors removed, the planet is now at the mercy of another Atlantean, the master scientist Sefner Quorne....

Book Four: *The Amethyst City*

The metaphysical union of the Amazon and Abna results in the mental creation of a fully mature daughter— Viona. Quorne, still struggling for domination, forces Viona into a marriage ceremony, and impregnates her. But with the intervention of Tarnec Brodix, a super-mind from an external universe, Quorne and Viona are separately flung into an ultra-dimensional limbo. Abna chooses to follow after his daughter, leaving the Amazon to brood over the disaster, alone in the Amethyst City of Saturn.

Book Five: *Daughter of the Amazon*

A miscalculation by the super-mathematician Tarnec Brodix destroys his universe, and the fault spreads into the Earth universe in the form of a Dark Tide of Absolute Nothingness. Unable to save himself, Brodix transfers his knowledge into the one mind powerful enough to receive it: that if Sefian, the son who has been born to Viona and Quorne. Sefian rapidly evolves, and, no longer human, after saving the Earth universe, vanishes into the greater universe, to seek new challenges. Then the Amazon is confronted with a further puzzle—a large section of the planet Neptune is discovered to be an exact duplicate of the Earth!

Book Six: *Quorne Returns*

The bacterial intelligences of Neptune plan to conquer Earth by replacing humans in key positions with alien duplicates. The Neptunians are themselves subjugated by the sinister Atlantean scientist, Sefner Quorne. Alerted to the threat, the Golden Amazon hits back by creating the ultimate doomsday weapon—only to precipitate a reprisal from the denizens of another universe....

CHAPTER ONE
CASTAWAYS

A clear blue sky, the golden light of a yellow sun, and warm, entirely breathable air. Yet the world where these conditions reigned was not Earth: it was not even a world in the Earth universe at all, but a planet in a different plane of matter.

And here, on this remote speck in the seas of infinity, three people sat on a massive boulder and considered the complexities of their position. Unexpected events had reduced them—from the perspective of the Earth universe—to microcosmic smallness. Near them the machine in which they had reached this alien world stood smashed almost in pieces, seeming to them in their small size to be as huge as a mountain.

For three ordinary people to be lost on this remote planet would have been hopeless; but these three were not ordinary. They probably represented the most brilliant scientific minds ever evolved in human form. One was the Golden Amazon, queen of the Earth Solar System; the second was Abna, once lord of Jupiter and now the Amazon's husband; and the third was their daughter Viona, supremely clever and massively strong, as were her parents, but having much of the thoughtlessness and lack of perception common to youth.

Surveying the desolate waste of rocky plain upon which the sunlight was pouring, Abna said: "We're lost in both time and space."

The Amazon turned to look at him.

"The problem is grim both for ourselves and Quorne," she said. "But we are probably better off than he is because we have each other. I cannot imagine anything more terrifying than to be alone on an unknown world with no apparent means of escaping from it."

Sefner Quorne, master scientist of Jupiter, had more than once tried to impose his will and powers upon other worlds, always to be beaten by the three who now sat on the boulder. There had even been a time when he had been married to Viona—and, in the legal sense, he still was. But destruction of her memory of Quorne's enforced union with her, which her father had mentally produced upon her, had made Viona oblivious to the fact that she was still Quorne's wife and had even borne him a son, whose very genius had destroyed him.

The immediate events leading up to the present predicament had been less sinister. A flaw in their space machine's power plant had reduced the trio on the boulder to smallness. Quorne, who had also been aboard the vessel, had stayed at normal size and the crash had not killed him. Where he was now was not certain. He had last been seen as a giant figure striding away with seven-leagued boots toward the horizon. He and the three on the boulder were sworn enemies and, until he or they were extinguished, there could never be peace.

"Quorne is huge; we are small," Abna said. "Whether that is an advantage or not, I don't know yet."

He stood up, as massive as a Grecian god with his enormous shoulders and—normally speaking—seven feet of height. Slowly he surveyed the dreary scene.

"Do you suppose there is life on this planet?" the Amazon asked, also getting to her feet.

"I have no more idea than you, nor can I see that it matters. Our sole problem is to find the way back home."

"I agree," the Amazon conceded, "but we might be immensely aided in that task if we could find intelligent scientists to help us."

Abna gave a rather grim smile. "Intelligent scientists, Vi? What do you suppose we are?"

"There is more assurance in numbers!" she retorted.

Viona rose and gave them a meaning look from her blue eyes. She was accustomed to these wranglings between her parents and, more often than not, was the means of subduing them.

"Between us," she said, "we are surely capable of solving our own problem? *You* are, father, in any case. You can make matter obey your mental powers when you try and—"

"I am perfectly aware that I can behave as a god when the occasion warrants it," Abna interrupted, "but

I am afraid this is too much even for me. Think what is involved! Time, space, subatomic dimensional wormholes—the whole vast mathematical complexity. Don't you recall that before the machine crashed we had the computers at work trying to determine for us the way home—?"

"Which they would have done had there been time," Viona interrupted.

"True—but they were machines, and infallible. I am flesh and blood and liable to inaccuracy."

The Amazon sighed. She gave Abna a reproachful glance from her unfathomable eyes and then looked at Viona.

"Your father is behaving like a schoolboy again, Viona," she said, shrugging. "He always does when he faces a crisis, and I'll never understand why."

Abna grinned. "Too much exercise of godlike power destroys the desire to be human," he explained. "And if I no longer felt human, I'd cease to love you and Viona...then where would I be?"

"Look!" Viona said sharply, pointing.

Her mother and father turned, and stood gazing at the incredible vision of an approaching figure. He appeared as big as a cathedral, so immense that his head and shoulders were lost to sight in altitude. Feet that shook the ground, and which seemed as big as double-decker buses, came steadily forward. It was Sefner Quorne, still in his space-boots and close-fitting flying-kit.

Quickly the minimized trio scuttled out of the way

of the behemoth boots, and then close beside each other waited to see what Colossus would do next. He, unable to detect them, since from his point of view they were less in size than the point of a needle, turned and strode toward the "mountain range" which was actually the *Ultra*, the wrecked time-space machine. When he reached it he became busy amidst the debris, shifting great sheets of metal that clanged so violently to the watching three the sound waves threatened to split their eardrums.

"Looks to me," the Amazon said, "as though he's already explored this world and not found anything on it. How big do you suppose this planet is?"

"Not large...." Abna seemed to be musing over something else. "If we were normal size, we could probably circumnavigate it in a reasonable time. As it is, it would take us about as long as walking around the Earth.... Materials are densely packed, obviously, for, despite this world's smallness, Quorne isn't walking lightly. Which means dense matter."

"It looks to me," Viona remarked, "as though he is trying to patch up the *Ultra*. Not that I can see it will be any use to him if he does. The computers must be wrecked, and they are the only instruments which can work out the formula of infinite expansion necessary to get back to our normal universe."

"Quorne," the Amazon replied, "is probably repairing the *Ultra* so he can have somewhere to live. He can also possibly make it void-worthy, which means he can travel to various other worlds until perhaps he finds one that is inhabited. There he may settle until he can solve how to get back home."

"Best thing for us to do," Viona said, "is to let him get the *Ultra* fixed up, then go inside it and travel to wherever he decides. We'll never be seen, though we also have the problem of food and drink to cope with."

"True," the Amazon said. "What do you think of the suggestion, Abna?"

He was studying one of the instruments with which his waist-belt was adorned. When he spoke he did not answer the Amazon's question. Instead he said: "This high frequency detector responds to Quorne. Look at the needle: it is following his every movement."

The Amazon gave an impatient glance. "What of it? We can see where Quorne is without a detector...."

"There's only one explanation for this," Abna continued, lost in speculations. "Quorne was originally expanded to infinite size by Molith of Ur, was he not, in an attempt to destroy him? Then by a mistake our computers brought him back again. It can only mean that the original energy expended upon him by Molith's apparatus has been absorbed by him, so strongly that it affects this high-frequency detector. In other words, wherever Quorne may go we shall always be able to approximate his position by means of this detector."

"Yes," the Amazon agreed. "Now, will you please answer my question? Should we go aboard the *Ultra* and go wherever Quorne goes? Remember our purpose, to destroy him, is still unfulfilled."

Abna put away the detector and stood thinking, his

keen eyes on the Goliath who was busy in the wreckage of the *Ultra*.

"To just fly around as minute stowaways from one world to another is not my idea of fun," Abna said presently. "Besides, in our present size we can never defeat Quorne. We cannot handle a single instrument because we're too small."

The Amazon said: "We must have nourishment and shelter. Also, we have no guarantee that the climate of this planet will always be as calm as it is now."

"All of which I have taken into account," Abna responded. "It seems that for once in my life I have got to abandon all material methods and turn to pure thought to get us home. I hadn't wanted to be bothered, but apparently there is nothing else to do." He settled down again upon the boulder and pondered. "I'll have to work it out. When I have done so, I'll tell you what to do. Don't interrupt me."

CHAPTER TWO
ERROR OF JUDGMENT

This was a command that the Amazon and Viona promptly obeyed. Both of them knew the astounding mental feats Abna could perform when necessary, but always he needed time beforehand in which to map out his plan of action. So as he sat brooding, looking very much like Rodin's statue of the 'Thinker', the two women took it upon themselves to watch the giant figure of Sefner Quorne as he worked on the shattered *Ultra*. It so happened, however, that everything was patterned on such a gargantuan scale they could not determine what Quorne was doing. Finally, they gave up the attempt, driven away chiefly by the stunning noise created by the shifting of metal plates.... Only one factor seemed to emerge from the chaos: by degrees Sefner Quorne was using the *Ultra*'s many machine tools to repair the heavy damage that had been wrought.

Abna, for his part, was hardly aware of what was going on around him. So completely was he able to detach his mind from immediate events, he was already oblivious to them. Instead, he was mentally exploring formula after formula, integrating the complex weavings of spatial mathematics necessary to bring about a return to the ordinary Universe—or at least the Universe that he, the Amazon, and Viona understood.

And, in assimilating the mathematical currents, he started for himself the longest mental analysis he had ever undertaken. Hour after hour he sat as though petrified, his eyes closed, his body so detached from his thought he neither experienced cramp, nor needed nourishment. Now and again the Amazon and Viona looked at him, then at each other, but they kept quiet. Once, when hunger and thirst became too much for them, they explored the mighty ruins of the *Ultra*, avoiding Quorne's titanic feet, and from the shattered food compartments removed a few crumbs that, for them, were as satisfying as full-sized loaves. For liquid they stood under one of the broken water vents and allowed the fluid to drop into their mouths.

A week passed and worry, for the two women, was at its height, when at last Abna stirred and looked at them. He might only have been thinking for a few seconds for he said calmly: "Yes, we can get back."

"Will it be difficult?" the Amazon questioned.

"For me, yes; for you two, no. I shall be obliged to carry you along under my own mental impulse, for neither of you have the intelligence required to work alone."

The Amazon did not say anything, but her beautiful face hardened a little. Then she relaxed again; knowing only too well her limitations, when Abna exerted his full powers.

"You'll be hungry by now," Viona said. "We got a few crumbs from the *Ultra* and—"

"Thanks, my dear, but I'm not hungry." Abna gave her a mystical smile. "Feasting upon intelligence wipes out all material sensations and desires.... Ah, I observe Quorne is progressing with the *Ultra*! It even looks to be taking on its former shape."

"It is," the Amazon replied. "He seems to have about restored it. If we ever get back home we'll have to build another *Ultra*."

"We'll get home all right," Abna promised. "And we'll start now. Come and sit beside me, both of you."

The two women sat as directed, and he laid one hand on each of theirs.

"All you have to do is submit passively to my thoughts," he explained. "They will presently control your minds, much in the manner of hypnotism, though this is actually a very different thing. Do not mentally struggle in any way: by degrees you will lose consciousness of your bodies, just as if you were under an anaesthetic, but you will be aware through mental currents of everything that is happening about you. Just leave me to guide everything. It is a supreme test of mind over matter. Now, are you ready?"

"Ready!" both women assented together, and closed their eyes.

They knew there was nothing fantastic about what Abna intended doing. On numberless occasions in the past he had revealed himself the absolute master of material conditions, so there was no reason why he should not reveal the same power again.

And, suddenly, the overwhelming force of his concentration made itself felt. Though their eyes were shut, the two women saw quite clearly, presumably through his own focused mind-forces. The barren little world was already flying away from them in a soundless rush of speed. They were in space, unaware of their bodies, unaware of anything except a deep peace and irresistible velocity.

By all scientific standards they were, the Amazon judged, moving faster than light—which was quite possible, she realized, since thought is not limited to the velocity measurements of normal radiations. And, since the minds were traveling, so were the bodies. On and on, faster and faster, through soundless emptiness.

Upon the Amazon and Viona there presently settled a dreamy contentment such as they had never experienced in their lives before. They felt entirely secure, embraced as they were in the grip of Abna's stupendous and yet tender mentality. And he himself, with all the courage that he had always displayed, concentrated further and further, deeper and deeper, using now every mental trick he could think of to overcome the huge mathematical and spatial distances involved.

The atomic universe fell away like dream shadows. Stars and nebulae gyrated. Vast unrelieved blackness swept in, in the midst of which there was only that eternal conviction of stupendous velocity. Then, very gradually, it began to slacken. The feeling of well-being wore off. The Amazon and Viona both realized that they had bodies again, that they were breathing with difficulty, and that they were lying on their backs on something extremely hard.

They opened their eyes.

At first they had the impression they were still upon the barren world. There was the same rocky, friendless plain. But here similarity ended. The sky was black, not blue—and it was not black because it was night, for a vast sun was lying bisected by the jagged horizon. A sun red and dull and swollen, from which life was obviously dying away.

The atmosphere was viciously thin and cold, making it an effort to draw breath. Three normal human beings would probably have suffocated or frozen, but because the trio who now staggered to their feet had super-human resistance, they managed to survive, and look about them, and wonder.

Their impression on every side was one of infinite loneliness. Not a living thing anywhere. And out of the north a howling wind came suddenly, bringing with it small spears of icy snow. Then it cleared again and the relentless stars were blazing as before.

"What—what's happened?" Viona asked, baffled. "Where are we, father? Did we make the trip back, or didn't we?"

"We made it all right." Abna was looking about him. "But I suppose I can be forgiven for not exactly timing the point of our arrival. It's pretty clear what has occurred. We've come back to Earth, but at a period in its remote future, instead of when civilization was at its height, which was the time we departed from."

The Amazon said: "Yes, the last days of Earth. The planet is motionless with one face to the sun, slowed down at last by incessant tidal friction. The air is dying out. Even the sun is waning. And all civilization is long since crumbled into dust. We've come back, Abna, but to a dead world."

"Yes," he said simply.

The women did not question him.

"Yes," Abna repeated quietly. "I'm sorry. Very inaccurate of me.'"

"It's done," the Amazon said, "and we have to get out of it. I assume that since you succeeded in lifting us out of that alien universe via atomic space, you can also overcome this present error of judgment? We certainly can't stay here. The cold is too intense and the air too thin. And we have no food.... For a while we can survive, perhaps, but in the end—"

Abna nodded. "Obviously, we cannot stay," he confirmed. "I must meditate again."

"At least we've ditched Quorne at last," Viona remarked to her mother. "He's in another plane of matter, and I doubt if he'll ever have the brains to get back."

"I wish I could be sure of that," the Amazon muttered. "Of Quorne we can never be sure until he is destroyed."

"True, but there is a way of keeping him within our grasp—literally," Abna remarked.

The two women turned in surprise. They had thought he was concentrating, but apparently he had finished this task, for he was coming over to them.

The Amazon caught at his arm.

"Well, can it be done?"

"You mean get back to our own time? It means working contrary to accumulation—which is advancing time—and I'm not able to do it. You cannot move backwards in Time."

Viona said: "We can't stay here!"

Her father shrugged. "Afraid we'll have to until we can think of something else. We might mentally create shelter and food for ourselves: that wouldn't be too difficult. After all, I did create an entire city on Saturn."

"That isn't the point," the Amazon insisted. "I don't doubt you could create a city here if you wanted, but what good would it be to us without the company of others? Without the means to explore; without natural things around us?"

CHAPTER THREE
BACK HOME SAFE AND SOUND

Abna refused to be disturbed. As was his custom after a supreme mental effort, he had become almost schoolboyish, glad to relax completely and throw all his troubles overboard.

"About Quorne," Abna said, glancing at Viona. "I think we have a way of keeping tabs on him! In our journey from the subatomic wormhole we traveled in a straight line, constantly expanding as we moved until we assumed our present normal size. Since we did move in a straight line, Quorne must be somewhere in the air about us, or at least the sub-atomic gateway to the universe in which he is existing will be.... Let me see now."

"Can't we forget Quorne for the moment and concentrate on ourselves?" the Amazon demanded.

"Knowing Quorne's capabilities, I don't think we can ever afford to forget him." Abna took the high-frequency detector from his belt and pressed the release button. Then he smiled as the indicating needle swung and presently became steady, pointing horizontally at nothing in particular.

"Still on him!" Viona exclaimed. "Over all that distance!"

"Distance is relative," Abna told her. "Our own extreme smallness made the distance seem of staggering proportions. A moment, while I work out some mathematics. I can then tell from this detector exactly where Quorne is."

That the two women were far more interested in their own fate than Quorne's Abna knew full well, but he refused to be turned from his purpose. Regardless of the icy wind, he worked out his mathematics with the tiny portable computer in his belt, and then gave a smile.

He said: "The atom of argon, in which lies the wormhole gateway to the universe in which Quorne is stranded, is seventeen feet four inches away from us where the needle is now pointing. Our atmosphere is partly made up of argon, as we know, and that is the point from which we came. We can suck a sample of air into an ampule, which will contain that one argon atom we want—which contains the wormhole entrance to that other universe from which we came—and we can keep the air, and Quorne, sealed in the ampule for as long as we wish."

"Yes, that's true enough," the Amazon agreed, impressed by the simple and yet mighty scientific fact Abna had stated.

From his belt Abna took an air ampule and then, with a spring rule carefully measured the distance of seventeen feet four inches from the detector, which he placed upon the ground. This done, he made some more calculations, then into the ampule he drew a specimen of air and sealed the top.

"Viona, watch that detector," he instructed, and the girl obeyed. He then proceeded to walk in a circle round the instrument, the air ampule in his hand.

"The needle is pointing to you," Viona told him. "Everywhere you go the needle goes too."

"Which means success," Abna smiled. "The needle is following the ampule, not me. Quorne is safely 'imprisoned', indirectly, within this tube. Apart from that one valuable argon molecule there are millions of others—but that is beside the point. We have Quorne all bottled up, and we'll be fools indeed if we ever let him out!"

With that Abna put the ampule carefully away in the protective slot in his belt, and then pondered and looked about him. Then Viona said: "You wouldn't think me impudent, dad, if I made a suggestion to get us home, would you?"

Abna laughed. "My dear girl, if you've any bright ideas, then let us have them!"

"It's a simple idea. Since we can't go backwards in time—what's wrong with going forward?"

"We could do it," Abna assured her. "Just as easily as we came from the atomic space—"

"But it would be of no benefit," the Amazon insisted. "The Earth and sun are dying even at this stage: to go forward would only make that fact more certain. We'd finally find the world crumbling into cosmic dust, the sun a dead star, and ourselves floating in space prior to our own inevitable annihilation."

"So I think," Abna commented.

Viona said: "'I seem to remember a theory was once propounded by a scientist famous in his day—Jeans I think his name was—that worlds have their own particular time orbit, independent of the great sea of time in which all the universe moves."

"Meaning what?" the Amazon asked.

"Meaning that maybe when Earth has come to the end of her time orbit, she starts all over again from the beginning. Why not? That is the basis of the Cyclic Universe theory, namely that all universes die out and renew themselves from pent-up cosmic forces—just as the cycle of nature everlastingly repeats. Death in the fall and renewal in the spring. Since we can't go backwards, we might as well try going forward and see if we don't find ourselves at the start of the circular Earth time orbit again."

"Having a definite logic," the Amazon said, "I think we ought to try it."

"Agreed," Abna nodded. "Let us start. Traveling forward will not be nearly so difficult to integrate mentally as that journey from Smallness. Stand here beside me, link your hands in mine, and I'll see what I can do."

So for the second time Abna once again threw every vestige of his immense intellectual power into the problem—and as before he and the two women gradually became dissociated from all consciousness of their bodies while their mental eyes remained wide open.

As though they were omnipotent observers, they saw Earth speed onwards in time until it was a dark and frigid world, caked in ice from pole to pole, the last rays of the fading sun casting back redly from it. And ere long, even these rays ceased as the sun became a burned-out star.

With the endless progression of time, even the dead star crumbled into a black hole, and there was nothing but the eternal cosmos and the blaze of stars and nebulae. Then, for the disembodied three, there came a brief sense of tremendous strain that quickly passed. All three of them knew that they had crossed the barrier at the end of the Earth time-circuit, had reached its absolute maximum, and that beyond it in the everlasting circle must lie the conditions known as advancing time. They had come back to the beginning of the circle and were still going forward.

For a while nothing changed on the face of the cosmic deeps, then out of remoteness a swirling nebula swung into view moving with a stupendous velocity. Probably its apparent velocity was so tremendous because of the speed at which the mentally traveling three were hurtling. Whatever the exact factors involved, they were the witnesses of enormous concentrations of incandescent gases contracting in upon themselves, forming into distinct stellar systems.

Space was white and trembling, shivering with inconceivable radiations and forces as the several of these proto-stars collided in the cosmic maelstrom.

One of the outflung flaming fragments was seen to coalesce into one stupendous dark island.... But it was now no longer dark. It flamed, coalesced, liquefied into blinding grandeur as its latent atomic powers were imploded by stupendous gravitational forces.

Perhaps ages passed, which the disembodied three could not calculate, but they saw the several ring-like filaments break away from the central core, whirl, and then condense into globes and slowly cooling worlds. They no longer needed to wonder if they had made the correct move. The proof of it lay there before them. They were even now speeding across the period of the Solar System's birth, so inevitably they saw the planets cool off, give birth to moons in most cases, and follow the inevitable law of the time-circle thereafter.

Abna changed his concentration somewhat so that the three found themselves apparently on Earth itself, and yet apart from it and untouched by the furies and storms of those very early days. They beheld tempest and hurricane, sunlight and calm. They swept through the kaleidoscope of hurtling ages, through the forests and swamps of primeval time, through the Glacial Epochs and Antediluvian ages.

Onward and onward to the first remote signs of civilization, and then the blur of the speeding centuries wherein man rose to a zenith and crumbled down again. Lost in antiquity became the epoch of the Egyptian dynasties and, instead, modern civilization was already growing. So through the ages of steam, of water, of the first flights, through the chaos and confusion of wars, beyond the Atomic age and the smashing of the sound barrier; still on to the age of the interplanetary travel, to the era of the Golden Amazon and her rule of the System.

And, suddenly, journeying ceased. The Amazon and Viona both realized at the same moment that they were standing on a high rise of ground to the north of modern London. Abna was near to them, smiling in triumph.

"You were right Viona," he said. "The Time-circle is continuous, and here we are right back in the period from which our adventure into Smallness began.... It seems to me it is time we went home and considered the vastness of the thing we have accomplished."

CHAPTER FOUR
STRANGE ACTIONS FOR VIONA

They returned home quietly and without attracting undue attention. Here and there a passerby immediately recognized them, wondered perhaps at their travel-stained appearance, but did not ask questions. Since the Amazon and Abna represented Earth and the System's center of government, no interrogation of them could be countenanced.

So they came back to that strange house in outer London—the great residence with the photoelectric pillars down the driveway and the curious aerials and scientific detectors on the roof.

The door opened before their combined thought-waves and then relocked itself as they passed into the lounge from the hall.

The Amazon spoke first.

"Throughout my career home has never meant anything much," she confessed, "but this time it is different. There is something wonderful about returning to it after twice thinking we'd never see it again. And it is all owing to you, Abna. I'm not a very grateful person as a rule, but this time I do thank you for all you've done from the bottom of my heart:"

"Nothing at all," Abna grinned. "Blame it all onto our erring daughter here. She thought of it."

Viona did not answer. She was sprawled on the divan, her copper-colored hair tumbling about her shoulders, a far-away and curiously puzzled light in her blue eyes. She did not even appear to hear her father's comment—until he directly addressed her.

"What's the matter, Viona? Falling asleep?"

"Oh, no! Sorry!" She straightened up and gave her mother and father a queer glance. "Just something I was thinking about.... Time we had a meal, isn't it?"

She went over to the radio button, which would automatically set a meal into the process of preparation in the domestic regions. To the Amazon it was more than plain that Viona had thought of the meal as a means of preventing any more questions being directed at herself.

"Home, sweet home," Abna murmured, relaxing his great frame into the armchair. "I suppose there are times when it is useful to behave as a god—but I hope I never have to do it again. It becomes wearing."

The Amazon did not comment. She was watching Viona. The girl had strolled to one of the great windows and was looking out absently into the grounds, the sunlight emphasizing the slender strength of her young figure in the slacks and blouse. It was more than plain that something was on her mind, or else she had not yet fully recovered from the awe-inspiring mental journeys that had been made.

Then a robot entered the big room, bearing a tray filled with food, drink, and table necessities. In a matter of minutes a perfect meal had been set out and the robot—responsive to their thoughts—went about its next task of cleansing the hands and faces of the three with a powerful, sweet-smelling detergent.

Refreshed, the Amazon and Abna rose and crossed to their places at the table, but Viona still lingered by the window, lost in speculations.

"Time to eat, sweetheart!" Abna called, and at that Viona glanced and then looked away. When she finally took her seat at the table, it looked as though she were deliberately trying to avoid looking at her mother and father.

"Anything wrong?" the Amazon asked.

"No," Viona said, and went on eating slowly.

"Then why so silent?" Abna questioned, surprised. "As a rule you behave like me...clean crazy. Or so your mother thinks, anyway."

"I—I don't feel like eating," Viona said abruptly, getting to her feet. "If you'll excuse me, I'll get some rest. I'm worn out."

"So are all of as," the Amazon remarked, "but we still need food. Get on with your meal and don't be so silly."

Viona gave them a hard look, which was unusual for her. Then without another word she left the room.

Abna remarked: "Perhaps I said something to her which she didn't like, but I can't remember what."

"It's not that." The Amazon shook her head slowly.

"I know her better than you do, Abna, and there's something deep inside her mind upsetting her. And, judging from the look she just gave us, we're mixed up in it somewhere."

Abna said: "I could read her thoughts if I wanted and find the cause of the trouble, but I don't think I'm entitled to do it."

So the conversation drifted into normal channels and. presently, the meal was over.

"Next, rest and plenty of it," Abna said. "But let me make sure our old friend, Quorne, is well and truly locked away, then I can retire.... And you look as though you need sleep, too."

"I am tired," the Amazon admitted, pressing the button for the robot to clear away the meal; then she stood watching as Abna took the air ampule from his belt and placed it carefully on top of the grand piano. Moving away to a short distance he studied his detector and then nodded.

"Still registering," he said. "Which means that, despite our journey, and the vicissitudes of time and space, Quorne is still bottled up in the other plane. Better put him in the laboratory safe and forget all about him—or, rather, take a reading of him every now and again to make sure he isn't finding a way back."

"Our time journey, then, changed time for that air ampule as it did for us?" the Amazon asked.

"Obviously, since it traveled us."

Abna put the detector away then, picking up the ampule, left the room with it, returning in a few moments from the laboratory.

"Which settles that," he announced. "It's in the safe and since only you, Viona, and I know the thought-formula for the safe lock, Quorne is well and truly bottled.... Now, how about some rest?"

On their way along the upper corridor the two paused for a moment outside Viona's room, listening. There were no sounds.

"Should I look in on her?" the Amazon asked. "'Tell her that we're going to get some sleep?"

"And probably disturb her own repose to advise her of the fact?" Abna shook his head. "No, Vi. Let her be."

So they continued to their own room, unaware that Viona was certainly not asleep, nor, indeed, had she made any attempt to relax. She had changed and bathed and, at the moment, was busy combing her hair and considering her reflection in the mirror, not for reasons of vanity, but with the in-seeing look of one still lost in profound and somewhat unpleasant meditation. Finally she surveyed herself in her maroon corduroy slacks and red space-shirt; then she opened the bedroom door slightly and stood listening.

Gliding out into the corridor, she moved to the bedroom doorway where her parents slept. They were quiet, and Viona went silently downstairs into the lounge and across to the wall safe. Opening it, she looked inside, her expression darkening as she did not see what she sought.

Closing the safe, she reflected, then she headed for

the big laboratory at the rear of the residence. She was as well acquainted with the various apparatuses as her parents. Including the neat very short-wave radio detector, which by beam process, could pick up any voice anywhere in the world by a simple process of frequency and "personal aura" detection.

Going over to this instrument, she switched it on, set the indicator to her mother's aura number and then snapped the power button into place. After a second or two the voices of her mother and father came floating through from the bedroom upstairs.

"We'll probably find it monotonous, Vi, after all we've seen and done to just sit around and do nothing."

Long pause, then Abna spoke again: "In some ways I'm sorry there's nothing left to fight. I've no zest for humdrum things. With Quorne's exit point from that other plane bottled up in the laboratory safe, our last chance of an enemy has gone. Why don't we start an exploration of the remoter deeps beyond the solar system and—"

Viona switched off, her eyes bright. Hurrying across to the laboratory safe, she threw the unlocking thought waves against it and then quickly pulled open the door and took out the ampule. Carefully, she placed it in a soft bed of cotton wool inside a specimen case, locked it, then hurried with it from the laboratory and into the lounge.

Here she wrote a letter, propping it up where it could not fail to be seen. Then she left the house, still with the specimen case in her hand, and hurried over to her own garage. In a matter of minutes her completely silent atomicar was speeding down the driveway and she did not stop it until she had reached the Central London spaceport. Here she garaged the car and then headed for the executive offices, where Chris Wilson, a distant relation through law of the Golden Amazon, ruled the destinies of the great space lines.

"Hello, Viona!" he greeted, as the girl entered. "Many a long day since I've seen you—or your mother and father. How are you?"

Chris rose from his desk—a kindly-faced, white-haired man of still vigorous health, and probably one of the richest men on Earth.

"Fine, uncle, thanks." Viona gave him his courtesy title as she kissed him. "I've been away on a long voyage with mother and father—something connected with Quorne."

"Oh, him!" Chris Wilson made a grimace. "I hope he's out of the way for good. He's an infernal menace—or was."

"Also a very clever man," Viona said. "Anyhow, my reason for being here is to charter the best-equipped and fastest space machine you've got. And I want it immediately with a full load in the power plant."

"Oh? Why the urgency? And what's the matter with your mother's *Ultra*? Surely she'd loan it to you?"

"It's wrecked."

"Wrecked?" Chris looked astonished. "But how does—?"

"Please, uncle, I'm in a hurry," Viona pleaded. "I've

a very long voyage to make. So what can you do for me?"

Chris hesitated.

"Do your parents know about this projected voyage of yours?" he asked, switching through to the chief coordinator of space machines.

"Does it signify?" Viona asked. "I'm at an age to make my own decisions."

Chris shrugged, eyeing her, and then the specimen case in her hand. He seemed about to say something but the voice of the coordinator distracted him.

"Yes, Mr. Wilson? Coordinator speaking."

"I want the fastest and best-equipped space machine in the fleet moved immediately to the departure field. Viona Ray Brant will pilot it for herself."

"Very good, sir. The *XM-29* will be there immediately."

"Thanks, uncle," the girl said, turning away.

"Where are you planning to go?"

"I'm not quite sure yet, but certainly a long way from the Earth."

CHAPTER FIVE
REUNION WITH QUORNE

When she was on her way, Chris regarded the closed door for a moment, frowning to himself; then he crossed to the huge outlook window and surveyed the departure field. The *XM-29*, one of the very fastest pencil-shaped atomic-driven space flyers, was already being moved into position on its uptilted cradle, and presently Viona herself appeared, moving with lithe grace from the executive building.

Chris picked up the telephone and switched it through to the Amazon's home. But before he received an answer the *XM-29* was already commencing its diagonal flight into the morning sky.

"Yes?" Abna asked, awakened from slumber by the telephone at the bedside. "Yes, who is it? Abna speaking."

"Chris Wilson speaking, Abna. I thought you might wish to know that Viona has just been here and chartered one of the best space machines so she can make a long voyage."

"Viona has *what*?" Abna demanded—and across the room the Amazon stirred in her own bed.

Chris Wilson repeated his statement and gave the details.

"She took off a few moments ago," he added. "Gave me no hint of her destination and it certainly wasn't my province to ask."

"Right, Chris—and many thanks." Abna switched off and sat frowning.

"What is it?" the Amazon asked.

"Our erring daughter. She's chartered a spaceship and set off for a destination unknown—and without saying a word to us! That's a thing she's never done before."

The Amazon got out of bed and drew her robe about her. "This decision of hers to take a leap into space without telling us just doesn't make sense. Unless she's left a message rather than disturb us. I'll go and see."

She was absent no more than three minutes, then returned swiftly with Viona's letter in her hand. Her yellow face was grim and her eyes hard.

"Read this!" she said, and Abna took the letter and read:

> "When we decided to traverse the time-circle of Earth in order to return to our own day and age, there was something which you, father, evidently forgot! Memory of past things becomes restored when you cross again over a time already traversed.
>
> "I know that I am really the wife of Sefner Quorne, and that at one time I bore him a son. I can only assume that I forgot this fact because

you, father, did something to my mind. The fact remains that, whatever Quorne may be as a scientist and an enemy, he is still my husband and, as his wife, I owe him a definite allegiance. Certainly I cannot allow his eternal imprisonment in an air ampule.

"I realize that his restoration, if that can be brought about, might bring violent repercussions upon you and civilization at large, so I am traveling to a far distant planet, the location of which I am not stating, as I do not wish you to follow me, even though you have a detector on Quorne.

"I learned by the inter-radio of where the ampule was kept, and I have taken it with me. Why you ever tried to destroy my union with Sefner Quorne I cannot understand, but I certainly do not thank you for it.

"Goodbye.

"*Viona.*"

"Viona," Abna said gravely "is a little fool!"

The Amazon snapped, "Through a mistaken sense of loyalty to that devil she is actually going to try to restore him from via the microcosm to the everyday universe. Abna, we've got to overtake Viona. She can't have got far yet."

Abna was silent for a moment, then he laughed shortly. "I never thought of that angle, Vi—about recrossing time restoring an obliterated memory! No wonder Viona looked so sulky. Presumably she'd got her memory of Quorne back again and her loyalty to him as a wife blinds her to the villainy he has perpetrated.... Someday maybe she'll grow up."

"She'll be killed before then!" the Amazon snapped. "Quorne will show her no mercy if she brings him back. He's out to kill her as much as he is you and me."

She began to dress in her black space attire. Abna watched her languidly.

"Well?" she demanded. "Aren't you coming, too?"

"No, Vi," he, said. "For one thing we have no space machine capable of overtaking her— We have no *Ultra*, remember—and for another Viona is never going to mature until she has fought her own battles and learned through bitter experience just whom she can trust and whom she cannot. Once before in her life she had Quorne's character exposed to her, but evidently the lesson was not strong enough, or else her memory of it is not complete...." he broke off as a thought struck him. "Quorne kept her in some kind of hypnotic thrall when he first forced her into marriage, to blind her as to his real character. It's possible that in recrossing time, this delusion has been reawakened in her mind, and—"

The Amazon broke in impatiently: "And what of the danger to the whole universe if Quorne is restored?"

"If Quorne extends his influence beyond Viona to again try and achieve domination, then we're entitled to deal with him. Otherwise Viona must struggle by herself. It's her own choice—she must live or die by it."

The Amazon was silent. She had not the kind of nature that in any way revealed sentiment, but Abna who knew her so well could analyse her expression. With his usual deference he refused to read her actual thoughts.

"She hasn't gone forever, Vi," he said gently. "When she knows what a mistake she's made, she'll fight like a tigress to put things straight again, and nothing could be better for her. Be odd if, in the finish, Viona found a way to vanquish Quorne singlehanded, wouldn't it?"

The Amazon suddenly threw off her mood of despondency. "Very well, Abna, since she has taken this course, she must abide by it."

And while her parents were making up their minds to let her have her head, Viona was hurtling through space with ever-mounting velocity. Earth was already some 15,000,000 miles behind her, and, by all normal standards, she had reached the limit of acceleration which the human frame could stand. But Viona was not like a natural woman, any more than was her famous mother. She hid the strength of ten powerful men and stupendous resistance. So she piled power upon power, and the generating plant sang ever louder.

In order to be as far away from her parents as possible, Viona set the automatic pilot for Pluto, whose orbit was near the very rim of the solar system.

She relaxed on the pressure couch, set the alarms to warn of sudden danger, and then prepared herself for unconsciousness as the machine was left to mount velocity upon velocity until it had reached maximum and the fuel in the power plant had burned itself out.

Upon Viona the darkness of oblivion descended, and an omnipotent observer could have glimpsed her machine streaking with awful speed through the empty reaches of space, until at last constant velocity was attained as the last shred of atomic power was wrested from the copper basis.

Viona opened her eyes, conscious of a tremendous lightness. Now acceleration had vanished and the speed was constant. There was no gravity as such. She lay for a moment assimilating the situation, then she lightly sprang from the couch and went to the nearest window.

She beheld the desolate, lifeless surface of Pluto, now showing an appreciable disk. Beyond the minor planet stretched a great infinity of stars and nebulae, and at varying distances she picked out Rigel, Aldebaran, Sirius, and Betelgeuse.

Viona turned quickly to the power plant—too quickly, for she forgot the absence of gravity and wasted several minutes turning slow somersaults. When at last she was right side up again, she put a new copper bar in the plant and switched on the current, using it negatively to cheek her soundless velocity through space. So, gradually, the 'brake' being on the space machine slowed down preparatory to landing on Pluto.

Viona was already aware from previous expeditions that Pluto was utterly lifeless—the terrain being made up of rocks, mountains, and ice. So it did not signify which part of the planet upon which to land. Indeed, since her main purpose was to find a way to release Sefner Quorne via the microcosm, she could have done it in the space machine, but that would have meant using up power to keep the vessel steady. She had to retain enough spare bars to enable her to return home if she became so minded.

So, by degrees, she piloted the machine down to the nearest bleak plain and came to rest within the shadow of a huge mountain range.

When at last the drone of the power plant ceased, Viona looked about her, Gravity felt more or less normal now, and outside ranged infinity—the mighty distant wastes of the Milky Way. For a moment the unutterable loneliness of space swept in upon her; then by a sheer effort of will she mastered the incipient melancholia and turned to the various instruments with which the machine was equipped.

Like all the latest modern flyers, it possessed numberless machine tools, instruments for making more instruments in turn, and with these Viona set to work. Knowing the basic principles of electronic expansion, and consequent enlargement in size of any material object, she set herself the task of constructing the apparatus necessary.

At last, her instrument for matter enlargement was complete. Since she had no means of knowing how much enlargement would be needed to accomplish her purpose, she donned a spacesuit and went outside, trailing cables from the vessel to her instrument. Finally she set it up some thirty yards away from the spaceship. Then she took the ampule from its specimen case and, without uncorking it in ease the valuable molecule of argon should be lost, she stood it up in a little cleft of rockery and then switched on her apparatus.

Immediately the current struck the ampule, it commenced to increase in size, and the increase remained constant—the ampule becoming larger and larger until it was six feet high. Soon it was twelve feet—twenty-four—thirty-six, and it had lost all the characteristics of an ampule and become instead, a cloudy, transparent pillar through which Viona could see the star-clustered sky. Some inner scientific instinct seemed to suggest to her that she still leave the current flowing, so she remained standing, watching intently through her helmet visor. And in time there was nothing left of the ampule but mist—and at length even this began to dissipate.

Then it was that Viona saw something. At first she thought it was her mother and father arriving—for there, apparently sweeping down from the heights, came the all familiar *Ultra*. In an instant Viona knew that she was mistaken. The *Ultra* had been left with Quorne and he had been repairing it! Then that could only mean that Quorne's vessel had already been bursting free via the microcosmic universe and so had been the first thing to emerge.

Quickly Viona switched off her instrument and kept her eyes fixed on the *Ultra* as it came down to the immense desolate plain. Then a space-suited figure appeared. He raised an arm in greeting as Viona moved forward.

When she reached him, her last doubts went. There was no mistaking the hatchet-faced man with the heliotrope-colored eyes and black hair visible behind the helmet glass. He gave the faintest of smiles and motioned to the *Ultra*—upon which, Viona noticed, a marvelous repair job had been performed—then he followed Viona into the control room and closed the airlock.

CHAPTER SIX
A THREAT TO THE UNIVERSE

In a few minutes they had both removed their space-suits; then they turned to look at each other.

"Thank you, my dear," Quorne said calmly, his purple eyes ranging over the girl's face. "I am glad to discover that you have such a malleable mind."

"Malleable?" Viona frowned. "How do you mean? Or have you been reading my thoughts? I went through all that enlargement process because I considered it my duty to do so. After all, you are still my husband."

Quorne smiled icily. "So nice of you to remember it! And you surely do not imagine that you performed such advanced science of your own volition, do you? You do not for one moment think that your desire to help me was because you are still my wife?"

"That was my reason!" Viona insisted, but a little hesitancy had come into her voice.

Quorne shook his dark head. "Everything you did, Viona, you did because I willed you to do so!"

"That couldn't be so, Sefner. You see, in returning along the Earth timeline to the present day I—"

"You recovered your memory and found how

completely your meddling father had tried to destroy our union? Yes, I know all about that and I have known about it for some time. It was when I detected that had happened that I decided to use you.'"

"Use me?" Viona repeated blankly.

Quorne motioned to the softly sprung chairs. "Be seated, my dear."

Viona sank down in the nearest chair, but Quorne remained standing. There was something vaguely unnerving to the girl about his placid smile and the hard light in his piercing eyes. Before he spoke again, he put away the spacesuits, poured a drink of restorative for himself, and then strolled back to where Viona was seated. She watched him fixedly, half afraid, all her own preconceived ideas about this restored union now crumbling around her.

"You have a lot to learn in scientific tricks, Viona," Quorne stated at length, considering her. "You are still very young, and because of that your mind is pliable and easily assimilates orders.... Let me explain what happened. Your father, Abna, being the clever scientist that he is, absorbed the microcosmic gateway to the universe in which I was situated into an air ampule. You may ask how I could know that when, theoretically, I was a vast spatial distance away from him?"

"How did you know?" Viona asked.

"Through your mind, my dear." Quorne gave a crooked smile. "Since you were aware of your father's action, it was naturally recorded in your mind—and I, in sympathy with your mind, was aware of the fact.

You must remember that space is no barrier to mind and thought waves, because neither of them fall into the category of what we call a material manifestation, such as light waves, radiant energy, and so forth. From the moment you were reduced to smallness before the *Ultra* crashed, I was in touch with your outflowing thought-waves perpetually. That is why I say you are inexperienced. Your parents know how to mask their minds and render them unreadable, but you are too inexperienced to do that. I knew exactly what you were thinking about and, indeed, the fact that your father carried the air ampule along with him—and that you were close to him—rendered the receptivity of your thoughts all the easier for me. When you received back your memory of our earlier association, I became aware of it and decided to turn it to account."

"Do you mean," Viona asked, "that I obeyed your will in releasing you? That it wasn't my own idea?"

"That is just what I mean." Quorne sat down, his thin hands dangling between his knees, his eyes on the girl's face.

"'I—I can hardly believe it," Viona whispered, horrified. "I felt deep inside me that I owed you some kind of allegiance, that as your wife I could not allow you to be exiled in that alien universe and—"

"I think," Quorne broke in coldly, "that our association as man and wife was somewhat stormy, to say the least of it. Even Sefian, the product of our union, did not remain to bless us. He was translated into a mathematical abstract and forever disappeared. Allegiance to me! All you actually experienced were the impulses I put into your mind and, the stars be praised, you reacted without flaw. Here I am—and with the mightiest plan in my hands that any scientist ever had!"

Viona gazed at him blankly. "Plan?" she repeated vaguely.

"That's what I said! Time and again I have been defeated in my purposes by your father and mother, chiefly because I have always used basic scientific methods to enforce my will, which methods their scientific knowledge was profound enough to overcome. But now I have something very different."

This time Viona did not say anything at all; she was still endeavoring to grasp the grim predicament into which she had fallen. Quorne, as he had always done in the past, had again used her as his pawn, and this time there was no possible means of assistance—unless her father and mother had decided to rescue her.

"They won't, my dear." Quorne commented, reading her thoughts.

"Don't be too sure!" Viona retorted. "You have a certain energy within you which—"

"Yes, Viona, I know. It existed as long as I was in my former state, but now I have returned to normal, it has completely dissipated. No detector in the universe can ever find me now, so since your parents haven't arrived to look for their charming daughter, they certainly never will now. Get it through your mind that we're alone—completely alone. After all, that is what, you wanted, wasn't it, prompted by your loving emotions toward me?"

Quorne was smiling thinly, but the only light in his eyes was one of cold cruelty. Viona tightened her lips, and was silent for a long time, doing her best to confuse her thoughts, so that Quorne could not read the desperate fear that was striving to overcome her.

"You mentioned something about a mighty plan," she said. "Am I entitled to hear what it is?"

"Seeing you have become such a devoted wife, and also because I'll probably need an assistant, I have no objection to explaining my discovery. In a word, I believe I have discovered the radiations of the Central Intelligence, and if I have, it means I have also found a marvelous weapon."

"Central Intelligence?" Viona repeated. "I never heard of it, and my mother and father have never mentioned it."

"Your mother and father's researches do not interest me, Viona. I made my discovery while in the other plane, and I made it on these instruments in the *Ultra* here. It was sheer chance, I admit, otherwise the radiations would have been discovered long ago. Let me ask you a question. Where do you imagine intelligence comes from? Where do you think certain mental gifts spring from—such as scientific knowledge, great musical skill, and all the other talents? Whence comes memory, reason, and the kindred mental offshoots?"

"The brain, of course."

Quorne shook his head. "The brain is only the interpreter of the thought waves, just as a radio apparatus tunes in the waves of a central transmitter. Hence my designation of 'Central Intelligence'."

Viona sat forward in interest.

"In studying the various detectors in here," Quorne continued, "it occurred to me that since we definitely do receive all our knowledge and specialized gifts from a Central Intelligence, there ought to be some sign of it, so I adjusted several of the detectors into a much higher range than is normal, just to see what happened. I did it for the sheer sake of something to occupy me— and this is what I discovered. Come, see for yourself."

He rose and crossed to the switch panel and the girl followed him.

In silence she watched as Quorne threw in the main switch, then she surveyed the gauge needles swinging under the influence of unknown power.

"What you are beholding," Quorne said, "are the inflowing waves of intelligence from a central source whose position I haven't yet located. Just as light waves, ultraviolet, infrared, and so forth, all have their different place on the scale, so also have the varying degrees of intellect. At random one might say that here we see represented the waves of reason, memory, specialized gifts, and so forth, which every being with the correct brain equipment is constantly receiving and interpreting wherever they may be and no matter what planet."

"In which you wouldn't include certain types of animals and so forth?" Viona asked quickly. "They haven't the power of higher reasoning."

"Just so. That is why I said the 'correct' brain equipment. Do you not perceive the vast possibilities which lie here, Viona?"

She shook her head.

"Then I will tell you," he said. "Every radiation, physical or metaphysical, is capable of being deflected—or maybe 'dampened' is a better term. It is a problem in mathematics to determine the exact counter-radiation, but it can certainly be done."

Viona said: "With the physical waves, yes—such as ultraviolet, infrared, and so on. But with the metaphysical waves, no. If they spring from a central fount of intelligence as you say they do—and which I've no reason to doubt—you cannot possibly devise a counterwave because that would mean creating something intelligent yourself, and you can't do it! The Central Intelligence would never permit you to devise something detrimental to itself."

Quorne rubbed his slender hands together. "Viona, there are times when I have hopes for you," he said. "If only you were so wonderfully analytical all the time! But you are quite wrong, my dear. Metaphysical waves are still electrical at basis, though they are in a higher form than their counterpart physical waves. Thought waves can be detected on any physical laboratory equipment, as witness telepathy tests. Therefore, a higher form of electrical wave can be generated in exact opposition to a metaphysical wave and dampen its power, or even cut it out altogether."

"You mean you think you could devise dampening

waves to obliterate all the inflowing waves we see registered here?"

Quorne nodded calmly. "Just think what would happen, for instance, if the inflowing waves which are interpreted as memory were suddenly to fail! Suppose I deflected all waves from Earth that cause memory to function? How then?"

Viona stared at him. "But—but Sefner, that is going too far! It's tampering with the basic laws of the universe, of man's natural heritage! You can't do it!"

"I can, Viona, and I shall. And surely you are scientific enough to eschew such nonsense as natural heritage? The only things that rule man are scientific laws, and every one of them can be broken and set aside. I have it in my grasp to dam all the beneficent gifts—so called—of the Central Intelligence. With that power I can turn aside memory, reason, every worthwhile mental attribute, and reduce living beings to subservient mindless slaves for as long as I deem fit! And since the Central Intelligence must feed all the universes with its everlasting waves of intellect, I can subdue any part of any universe, prevent living beings wherever they may be from using their powers of reason or memory while I take control of them. Now you know why I said I had a mighty weapon!"

CHAPTER SEVEN
UNITED IN THE PLAN

Viona turned away, a feeling of sick horror taking possession of her. There was something in Quorne's audacious plan which revealed more clearly than ever before his devouring ambition and blasphemous egotism.

"What is the matter?" He strode across and seized Viona roughly by the shoulders, forcing her to look at him. "Can't your youth and innocence absorb the possibilities?"

"Youth and innocence have nothing to do with it, Sefner. And in any case, I'm far more mature than you believe. It is just that you're going too far. I'm convinced you are! You are not dealing with science: you are attempting to alter the course of Creation itself."

Quorne dropped his hands and sighed. "Earlier, for a moment or two, I had hopes for you as my wife. I even glimpsed the possibility of you standing beside me while I formed the Universal Brotherhood. Because of your silly sentiments, you are throwing aside the chance of being the queen of all the Universes, shoulder to shoulder with me." Quorne looked at her directly. "Between us, Viona, for my scientific skill can straighten the points you have yet to learn, we can make every living thing come under our control. We can bend the very intelligence of the universe itself to our desires. I shall do so in any case. Surely you are not going to stand aloof from that?"

Viona was silent again, following a variety of thoughts. She felt she could do so freely at the moment, for Quorne was now looking at the indicators again and making notes of their readings; he was far too absorbed to bother reading her mind. Which was just as well, for in the midst of her meditations an amazing thought came to her.

Unquestionably it must have come from the Central Intelligence itself, but in that particular moment such a possibility never occurred to her. All she realized was that she had the answer to her problem concerning Quorne, but to work her way to the solution would take time, disarming tact, and, above all, carefully shielded thoughts.

"I believe," she said, turning slowly, "that you are right, Sefner. I would be a fool to turn down such an offer as you have made!"

He glanced at her sharply, tossing aside the notes he had been making. She could feel the intensity of his mind as he probed into the depths of her thoughts, but so deeply buried—as yet—was her inspiration he had of hint of it. He read only a willingness to do as he wished.

"I'm glad you are sensible," he said briefly. "It seems

to me that the best thing we can do is behave as partners only, forgetting all the emotional issues which usually attend marriage. We bowed down to those issues before and achieved precisely nothing."

"Absolutely nothing," Viona confirmed. She moved to the control board. "What do you intend doing? Are you going to set up your dampening wave system from here?"

"No. But at the moment I am working out the mathematical details—determining precisely which wave is counter to which. It will be a long job."

"And when you have done that?"

Quorne mused. "I think we are going to need a space-island, contrived of transparent metal, so that it will be invisible to telescopic observers. Aboard the *Ultra* we have the necessary equipment for manufacturing such an island. However, first let me work out these figures."

And Quorne turned aside as though the girl did not exist. She watched him for a moment or two; then, finding little to interest her in the work he was doing, she got into her spacesuit. She was on her way to the airlock when Quorne looked at her quickly.

"Where are you going?"

"To bring my few possessions from that spaceship out there. I'm obviously not going to need it any more now we have the *Ultra* for both of us."

"You'll stay right here!" he snapped. "Do you think I am going to give you the chance of perhaps radioing to your mother and father that I am here?"

Viona shrugged. "I thought I had made it clear that I

am entirely loyal to you from here on?"

"Your loyalty to me has yet to be proven, Viona. Get out of that spacesuit."

Viona meekly obeyed and then sat down. It was not part of her purpose at the moment to show any resentment; nor indeed had she any. She felt absolutely confident of the plan she had worked out.

So for quite a few days—as measured by the chronometer—Viona prepared the meals and cleared them away; she saw to it that the control room was kept tidy. And throughout this time Quorne worked steadily at his mathematics, sometimes of his own accord and at others with the help of the computers, until, on the fourth day, his stack of notes seemed to satisfy him and he brought them across to the central table, where Viona was seated

"There it all is, my dear," he said, tossing the notes down. "A counter-wave for every radiation emitted by the Central Intelligence! All that is required now is the necessary machine to emit the counter waves. I have decided on one machine, able to alter its wavelength at the touch of a button. It will be a complicated task making it, but between us—for I shall want you to help me—there is no reason why we shouldn't accomplish our purpose."

Viona picked up the notes and glanced through them. She could tell at a glance that they were far too complicated for her to understand.

"You said something about a Universal Brotherhood," Viona remarked, putting the notes down again. "I don't quite understand your meaning. If it is your intention to subject everybody—reduce them to mindless slaves—where does the essence of Brotherhood come in?"

Quorne gave his hard smile. "It doesn't. It is merely a name. But all the same I believe that as we progress we shall bring into our orbit others of a like mind to ourselves—those who are willing to sacrifice everything for pure science and absolute domination. That will form the Brotherhood."

"Overlords would be a better term," Viona murmured, and Quorne gave her a flinty glance.

"Do not imagine," he said, "that those who have been bereft of their dominating faculties will stay like that indefinitely. By no means! I only intend to cripple the powers of reason, memory, and so forth, long enough to give me the advantage. After that the dampening radiation will be withdrawn and those who were under its influence will revert to normal, only to find that they are ruled by a power they cannot escape or overthrow. My power! And the instant there are signs of rebellion, back will come the dampening wave."

"And this influence is to extend throughout all the Universe?"

"By degrees, yes. It will be a lifetime of work, and when the time comes for me to die, as it must in the end, you will take over. By virtue of your being the daughter of the Amazon and Abna, you have their gift of almost eternal life—certainly life for 1,000 years, whereas my span is more or less normal. I cannot expect to last beyond 150."

"Which means you have decided to trust me with everything?" Viona asked quietly.

"By that time I shall know whether to or not. By that time I shall have extinguished your parents, and shall have crushed every dangerous form of opposition throughout the Universe. The Quorne Brotherhood will be established."

"To what end? So that you may sit on a golden throne and say, 'All this is mine'?"

Quorne slapped his hand on the table. "Why do you have to take that attitude?" he demanded. "Have you no spark of ambition at all, Viona? Have you no wish to use your great powers to a magnificent purpose? Don't you realize that you can have every being in the Universe crawling before you, doing exactly as you order? That, my dear, is exquisite bliss!"

"Depending on the point of view, Sefner. Personally I think it might prove boring. But that doesn't mean I won't support you. Maybe I'll catch something of the thrill of domination when I see how it works."

"Inevitably you will," Quorne told her. "The trouble with you, my dear, is that you have not been allowed to grow up. You have been constantly overshadowed by your mother and father, and they have seen to it that you stayed that way! Had you been allowed to have your head, you might have become a menace to their authority. You did wisely in striking out for yourself."

From that moment Viona followed Quorne's directions implicitly in the construction of a machine that she hardly understood. Even though she helped to build it and actually did some of the wiring, she was no wiser when, two weeks later, the instrument was finished, molded entirely by the *Ultra*'s machine tools. In height the apparatus stood eight feet and it was five feet wide. From top to base on one side—since it was box-shaped—there was a panel covered in switches of different colors; added to this were multiple banks of keys like those of an organ, together with row after row of dials. Within the instrument, so far as Viona understood it, was an atomic power plant.

"But that plant, of itself, is useless," Quorne explained, when it came to the final checking over. "It needs a constant, and inexhaustible power behind it, such as only the sun can give. Its distance from us does not signify, since its radiation can easily be amplified. I understand our own sun's powers in every detail."

"But once we go into space to establish the space-island, isn't there a chance our spaceship will be seen?" Viona asked, thinking.

"We can only be detected within 1,000,000 miles of Earth, my dear; otherwise, the *Ultra* is far too small to be picked up by normal telescopic observation. If we remain here, on the rim of the solar System, in space slightly beyond the orbit of Pluto, we will be sufficiently well hidden. And that is where I am thinking of establishing the space station. This instrument will have sufficient power, when the sun is the basic energy, to reach throughout the entire system."

CHAPTER EIGHT
FOR SAKE OF SCIENCE

Within half an hour the *Ultra* was rising from the surface of Pluto. The only sign of the visit lay in Viona's abandoned space machine.

Quorne headed the vessel in an arc, taking it to the very rim of the solar system. The disc of Pluto began to shrink. Beyond him ranged the giant outer planets and then, in steady inward orbital progression, Mars, Earth, Venus, and Mercury. The sun at this distance hung as a diamond-bright large star, but nonetheless his radiations were still powerful enough to power Quorne's apparatus after amplification.

"This," Quorne said, "is where we halt. At this point in space, we have a great deal of emptiness in which to mold our space-island."

He turned to the switchboard, slowed the *Ultra* down to an apparent standstill, and then came to the central table and spread out a blueprint.

"This," he explained, "is the island. There was once something very like it designed by your mother to protect Earth from invasion. I was present on it at one period and had the chance to study its details. Here it is, with elaborations."

The design showed a circular object, identical with a wheel, having an outer ring and 'spokes' leading to a central hub. In the ring were various control rooms and outlook observatories, and in the hub living quarters and the dampener, which, at the moment, was standing in the control room.

"We will make this object with the *Ultra*'s atomic patterning beams," Quorne explained. "You know how they work?"

"I should," Viona answered dryly. "Mother showed me often enough. They crystallize the radiations of space, hardening them from their ethereal quality until they take on matter form, after which their atomic constitution is altered to whatever is desired—iron, stone, glass, gold, or any desired substance."

"Exactly," Quorne agreed. "With the patterning beams we can make our space station, and once it is created, we will ensure that it remains in a fixed orbit. That is simple enough. The tendency of any big object like the space station will be to drift toward the solar system, due to the gravitation field. A beam of force projected at Pluto will stop the drift, the force being equal to the pull in the opposite direction."

"Clear enough," Viona assented. "When do we begin?"

"We have two patterners," Quorne said, glancing at them. "You man one and I'll handle the other. Follow my orders to the letter."

Viona nodded and crossed to the nearer instrument,

settling herself in the chair with which it was fitted. Then, peering into its eyepieces—as though it were some kind of television camera—she maneuvered it into the position stipulated by Quorne. In the 'viewscreen' loomed empty space, but after a while, as the power was switched on, this space became alive with seething energies as the invisible molding fingers began to form matter out of radiation—fusing it, hardening it, fashioning it.

Like all scientific tasks of this nature, not a great deal could be done at a time. For many weeks the *Ultra* remained 'anchored' far beyond Pluto, but during this time the central hub of the space-island took form— then came the radiating spoke tunnels, completely airtight, and finally the outer linked bridges that formed the periphery of the wheel.

Being close to the object, for it was not more than five miles distant from the *Ultra*, made it distinguishable, but for the sake of a test Quorne took the *Ultra* for a brief 200-mile leap and he and Viona looked back at the island to discover it had vanished. The translucent but immensely hard metal of which it was composed made space visible through it, and the material itself did not reflect light in any degree, so that unless one was almost on top of it, it defied detection.

Then back to the task again, holding it in position by magnetic beams from the *Ultra* until its own power unit could be equipped and check the drift toward the solar system.

Weeks passed. The space-island itself was finished,

and was followed by the task of using the *Ultra*'s machine-tool equipment to manufacture the necessary engines with which the island had to be equipped. Most of them were made sectionally in the *Ultra* and then ferried across the small gap of space with utmost ease, there being no deterrent gravity. Viona handled most of this task dressed in a spacesuit fitted with small jet recoils. In this way she could float about the abyss as she chose, punting the machine sections along as required.

Eventually the space-island was complete and all the machines linked up. There came a moment when the *Ultra* was brought alongside the hub of the island, anchored there magnetically, and Viona and Quorne stepped into their new "home" and laboratory to survey their handiwork. Certainly they had accomplished a masterpiece. They had an artificial gravity, and plenty of space in which to work; perfect air-conditioned rooms, laboratories, and living quarters, and particularly, any number of observatories on the outer rim of the wheel, wherefrom to view the void.... And in the hub stood the dampener, linked up now to massive power units, which constantly absorbed and stored the amplified energy of the sun.

"So," Quorne said, as he and Viona surveyed the central laboratory, "everything is ready. I trust you have grasped the beauty of this space-island, my dear? Obviously, to use the dampener throughout the universe it will have to be moved many times, since its effective range is limited to any one solar system. When we wish to use it in a different part of the universe we retire to the *Ultra*, take the island in tow and drag it wherever we wish. That is one advantage about space—weight is no detriment. Indeed, it ceases to exist."

"Your intention now is to dampen the waves reaching the Earth?" Viona asked, hut Quorne shook his head.

"First I have a test to make and a plan to work out. The Central Intelligence is situated, as near as I can work it out, at the exact center of the Universe. The Earth system is well to one side of that center. So I have to work out how to cut across a particular set of metaphysical radiations that are affecting Earth and, for that matter, all parts of the Solar System. I had thought, for experiment, that a space flyer might be the best. It will be bound to contain people with all types of minds."

"You mean one of those 'Curiosity Tours' that the Space Line runs? A trip around the solar system and back for sightseers?"

"Exactly," Quorne agreed. "There will be a large number of so-called intellectuals present among the passengers. Not that that is unusual, perhaps; only the higher type of mind would be interested in surveying space. However, be that as it may, a Curiosity Tour machine will make excellent bait. We must keep on the watch and then apply the Dampener. We shall know by radio reports how the passengers have been affected."

Viona merely nodded, not at all in favor of this idea of probably destroying an entire ship full of innocents for the sake of scientific experiment, but just at the moment she was quite unable to do a thing about it. Later, a chance would come, and then....

"Which metaphysical wave do you propose to dampen first?" she asked presently.

Quorne grinned. "The most dominant one of all, my dear—reason! It exists as number 11 on the scale and number 17 of my own counteractive beams should be sufficient to jam it completely, as one jams a radio wave. It will be interesting to note the effect if a crew and passengers find the gift of reason suddenly denied them.... Switch on the radio. We can tell from that when a Curiosity Tour is scheduled, and act accordingly."

Viona did as ordered. It was about this time, back on Earth, that a Curiosity Tour was just starting. They were more or less a regular service and were simply the ultramodern version of one-time coach-parties, but instead of a tour round the countryside or round the world, the Space Line offered a tour round the solar system. Thus it was that on this occasion, with no possible hint of the fact that they were being marked down by a sadistic scientist as his targets, 200 men and women, most of them of the leisured intelligentsia, embarked on the *Z-29*.

CHAPTER NINE
A VICTIM OF AMNESIA

The great lounge contained quite a sprinkling of celebrities: there was Harvey Kinson, the famous space artist, whose paintings of Jupiter had won him the highest honors; there was Lydia Dane, the famous woman composer whose *Symphony of the Worlds* had taken the Earth musical world by storm; and there was Barrington Lendar, a cosmic photographer, whose contributions of film to the world's observatories had helped to give a clearer insight as to the formation of the solar system.

These were only a few of the famous. Also present were the lesser lights, all of them apparently in a good humor.

In the control room Captain Henderson was in charge and, so far, everything was running to schedule.

"Routine can become very dull sometimes, Mr. Blake," he remarked to the astrogator.

"Yes, sir—very dull. I have hopes that my papers will soon be through for me to be transferred to the fast Earth-Mars run."

Presently Henderson said: "It occurs to me we're

drifting slightly off course. Just check your figures, Mr. Blake."

The astrogator studied his instruments, frowned, and then looked through the window.

"This may sound silly, sir," he said slowly, "but where are we heading?"

"Where?" Henderson stared at him. "Did you say where, Mr. Blake? Why to—to—"

The captain's voice trailed off and then stopped. He rubbed his forehead as though something pained him; then, like the navigator, he stared through the window. Everything out there seemed to be becoming cloudy and meaningless. It was quite impossible to focus upon intentions.

The astrogator looked quickly at his astral display. "It says Mars here, sir. Do you suppose that would be our next stop? Or is it Venus?" There was fright in his eyes now. "I think I'm getting amnesia, sir, or something. I can't seem to remember.... No, it isn't exactly that, either. I just can't co-ordinate things somehow."

"No more can I," Henderson whispered, still rubbing his forehead. "Call the psychiatrist immediately. Maybe he can explain it. Radiations have got us, perhaps."

"Radiations?" Blake gave a wild look, like a man who is about to drown. "What are radiations, sir?"

Henderson could not tell him, and they both already had forgotten that they intended to call the psychiatrist. Not that it would have been any good if they had. The psychiatrist himself was sitting before a stack of notes in his cabin, completely unable to reason out the thesis upon which he had been engaged.

In the lounge there were signs of trouble, too. Harvey Kinson, the great artist, was seated at the main window with a small easel before him. He had partly rough-sketched the distant moon and star background, but now his hand hesitated. He had not the vaguest idea what to do with the drawing he had started.

Because Lydia Dane, too, had lost her grasp of the fundamentals of musical construction, she sat frowning at the notepad on the arm of her chair, her expression one of complete vacancy. A similar expression was on the face of the cosmic photographer. He remembered he had intended to photograph something, but now he could not recall either the subject or the intricacies of his camera.

And the effect deepened with every second that the now uncontrolled space machine traveled onward. It was thousands of miles off course and, since the moon was at the moment the nearest body, it was pulling with ever greater power. Henderson knew there was something he ought to do, but he could not imagine what.

Two hours later radio news burst upon Earth that for some inexplicable reason the *Z-29* had crashed upon Mare Crisium without a single survivor. An Earth-Mars space liner had seen the incident and reported it, afterward making an investigation. As the head of the government, the report went first to the Golden Amazon, and she promptly issued orders for the captain of the Earth-Mars liner to be brought back to Earth with full details, a relief captain to take over in his place

Two hours after the *Z-29* had hit the moon, the Earth-Mars captain was in the Amazon's private office in the Chief Executive building.

"Sorry to break your journey, captain," she apologized, "but this incident is so extraordinary I want information firsthand. You say you saw the actual smash?"

"Yes. The *Z-29* cut straight across our path, very nearly ramming us. We made frantic radio signals but got no response. Down she went, straight into the moon, and later search showed she was splintered to bits."

"And no survivors?"

"Not one. In any event most of them were exploded by the sudden blast of air pressure. Not at all a pretty sight on the airless Mare Crisium, Miss Brant, I can assure you."

"I know," the Amazon responded, thinking. "When I first received your report, I took a look at Mare Crisium through the x-ray telescope and saw the details for myself." She frowned. "It is unbelievable! Apparently no effort was made to prevent the crash."

"That is how it would seem."

"Very well, captain, thank you. If you will report to base, you will be directed to a new vessel."

The Amazon called Abna on the visiphone. He was at the laboratory.

She said: "You have all the instruments in the laboratory there. See if you can detect anything amiss with space, anything which could cause a perfectly void-worthy touring liner to smash uncontrolled to the moon." She explained what had happened, and added: "I have some details to finish in the office here, then I'll go home."

When she returned home, Abna was waiting to report the results of his search. "Space is as clean as a whistle, Vi. The *Z-29* must have crashed for purely human reasons, but we'll probably never know what they were."

She said: "When something happens like this, I start thinking about Quorne."

"Yes, I see what you mean." Abna spoke slowly as he came to the Amazon's side. "For that matter, he could be still alive, I suppose. Though I'm inclined to doubt it. It must be getting on for nearly a year now since he failed to register on the detector, and at that time, according to my calculations, he was apparently heading out of the solar system."

"Which means Viona was also," the Amazon said. "She must have been, since she took the Quorne-ampule with her."

"I thought we'd agreed to let her fight her own destiny?"

"Yes, and now I think we must have been insane! I agree that she should fight her own battles, but when I realize that we let her take away Quorne with her—"

"But he must be dead, Vi! That is why he no longer registers on the detector."

"If he found his way back via the microcosm to

our normal Universe, he'll certainly be bending every ounce to consummate his plans for universal conquest."

"Then what do we do?" Abna asked. "We can't afford to go racing out into the deeps of space on the off-chance of locating Viona, and perhaps Quorne. If it should happen again, then we'll know it is not coincidence."

The Amazon was silent, a faraway look in her violet eyes. Abna put a great arm about her shoulders.

"You miss Viona, don't you?" he murmured.

"I do. The shadow of Quorne hovering over her makes me want to take off in *Ultra II* and try to locate her."

"You never would," Abna said gravely. "We've not a single clue upon which to work."

* * * * * * *

Aboard the space-island the news of the crashing of the *Z-29* had just been picked up over the delayed radio waves from Earth. Quorne was jubilant, and because it was all part of her plan not to seem antagonistic in any way, Viona did her utmost to appear enthusiastic.

"We have it, my dear; we absolutely have it!" Quorne declared. "We can dampen any particular outflowing metaphysical wave from the Central Intelligence and produce havoc by that very means."

"So it would appear," Viona agreed.

"Not a single survivor," Quorne mused. "How thoroughly the rot sets in when reason is destroyed. However, reason is if anything too powerful a thing to destroy: it wipes out too thoroughly. I think we might do better in dampening the waves relative to scientific knowledge. That will still allow the subject to reason clearly, but it will kill the memory of all things scientific. An excellent weapon to use against your mother and father, my dear."

"Excellent," Viona agreed mechanically—and Quorne gave her a sharp look.

"You are not relaxing into sentiment again, are you?" he demanded. "Haven't I made it clear enough to you that your parents have tried to prevent your reaching scientific maturity?"

"Yes, Sefner, you've made it clear enough—but they are still my parents. I cannot accept your threat of destroying them without showing some emotion."

"Emotions are for fools," Quorne snapped. "I shall make a few more tests and then decide on the best means of disposing of my—and your—sworn enemies. For the moment we can relax, but when we learn that another Curiosity Tour is about to start we will experiment further...."

And Quorne kept his word. The following day a Curiosity Tour machine beat a hasty retreat from the region of the moon's orbit and succeeded in landing back safely on Earth—but only because automatic devices had come into action. Upon investigation it was discovered—and indeed declared by many of the crew and passengers—that all recollection of scientific skill had disappeared during the journey, but had now returned.

*　*　*　*　*　*　*

That evening the Amazon called a meeting of the directors of the Space Line. Present among the normal officials were also Commander and Ruth Kerrigan, the original sponsors of the Space Line, Chris Wilson, and Abna. Abna was present not as a director but as co-partner to the Amazon in controlling the destinies of the Solar System.

"There is no doubt of one thing, my friends," the Amazon said, coming straight to the point. "Two such occurrences in the space ways cannot be called coincidence. I am inclined to suspect our old enemy, Sefner Quorne."

"I understood you to say he had been trapped in another universe," Chris Wilson remarked.

"I thought so until recently. Now I think I may have been mistaken. I intend to embark as a passenger on the next Curiosity Tour. I want it to begin tomorrow morning."

Wilson said: "The *H-67* should take off tomorrow. I expect most of those who have booked will turn up in spite of what has happened."

"I propose to take stop-action instruments with me," the Amazon said. "The moment trouble becomes apparent, I will switch them on, and, whatever the nature of the trouble, providing it falls into the laws of understandable science, it will be there for analysis afterwards upon the detectors. Always granting a return is made to Earth without a crash. That is one of the risks."

"I don't like it," Chris Wilson said uneasily. "We can't afford to lose you, Vi. Couldn't I go? I can be replaced if anything should happen to me."

"Commendable, Chris, but impracticable. I am the only one, except Abna, who can set the instruments."

"I had this matter of which of us should go over with my wife before coming here," Abna explained. "It is obvious that one of us has to stay and keep control over matters of the system, and when it comes to absolute analysis my abilities in science far exceed hers. More bluntly, if one of us has to be sacrificed, she preferred it to be herself."

"As always," Ruth Kerrigan commented, "you put science before personalities, don't you, Vi?"

The Amazon shrugged. "'I am taking what I believe to be the commonsense course, that's all. It is settled then? I shall embark incognito on the *H-67* tomorrow."

The assembly of directors nodded and the Amazon looked at Chris Wilson.

"Arrange for me to enter the machine through the crew airlock, then I can go straight to my suite and stay there. If I am recognized, there will be the usual annoying distractions."

At ten o'clock the following morning, nobody noticed the slim, apparently young woman in the neat two-piece, carrying a suitcase in one hand, who entered the *H-67* through the crew's airlock. The captain and astrogator stood to attention as she briefly acknowledged them, then she hurried through the emergency corridor to the private suite Chris Wilson had had prepared for her.

She set out her instruments on the bed, then she crossed to the fixed chair by the big outlook window and sat gazing into space as the *H-67* began its journey.

She pondered upon Viona and Sefner Quorne. She blamed herself for not following Viona while she had the chance. She meditated upon various topics as the *H-67* pursued its appointed course and was now beyond the orbit of the moon.

Then to the Amazon's brooding mind came the first sign of something amiss. At first she could not be quite sure what it was, then it occurred to her that she could no longer recall Viona, Quorne, or any of the details connected with her past life. She was not even aware of why she was aboard this machine.

With a tremendous effort she struggled to overcome the amnesia that was doing its best to defeat her. She got up from her chair and with the action she caught sight of the instruments upon the bed. For a moment the deepening cloud in her mind was pierced as she remembered the instruments' purpose. She almost dived at them and snapped on the various switches, and even as she did so, the last vestiges of memory whirled from her like vapors.

Trying to fathom what she was doing, and why, she opened the door of her suite and looked down the corridor. In the control room the captain and astrogator were visible, half sprawled in their chairs. The Amazon hurried in to them and looked in wonder at each man in turn. They were both conscious, but on their faces were blank expressions. Having less intelligence than the Amazon, not only their memories had gone, but most of their natural willpower as well. Dazed, the Amazon looked at the controls, but failed to remember how they functioned. This did not prevent her from seeing that a master-switch had closed into position, and above it was an illuminated panel saying "automatic control." No effort of memory was needed here for her to realize that the machine was perfectly safe, being guided by robot systems back to its starting point now normal control had stopped.

A sound behind her made the Amazon turn. In the doorway she beheld two massive rocket engineers, grime-covered and stripped to the waist. Their faces showed how completely they had been deprived of all natural control. With memory destroyed they had atavized to something approaching that of the beast. Evidently they had come from below, seeking whatever their debased instincts could find. And here was an apparently young woman of superb beauty, completely alone. Or as good as, considering the condition of the captain and navigator.

CHAPTER TEN
ON TO THEIR GAME

The first engineer lunged, aiming to seize the Amazon's shoulders. Though her own memory was in oblivion, she had at least the physical awareness of her superhuman strength—and so had the engineer a moment later. Her right fist slammed up into his stomach as he seized her, and in a sudden explosion of anguished breath he half doubled up. A terrific left hook under the chin made him straighten, and the third overwhelming blow the Amazon delivered smashed his jaw and sent him tumbling against the control room wall.

The second engineer came with a rush. At the identical moment the Amazon stepped aside and grabbed the nearest power lever, useless now the automatic control had taken over. With her steel-strong fingers she snapped the lever away from its ratchet, and then swung it down on the back of the second engineer's neck as he blundered past her. He fell to the floor with a broken neck.

Grim-faced and still holding the heavy lever as a weapon, the Amazon left the control room and hurried down the corridor to the main lounge. Here she burst upon a scene of absolute chaos. Shorn of all the memorized attributes of civilization and culture, men and women were engaged in battling with each other, or else were in the midst of an orgy of destruction. The costly fittings of the lounge were being torn from their moorings, chairs were being flung at the enormous mirrors; the furniture was being smashed against the walls.

The Amazon hesitated, not sure whether to interfere or not. Then as she saw a party of men whirling the grand piano along the floor, with the obvious intention of jamming two screaming young women against the wall, she intervened. Hurtling across the lounge she flung herself forward, ready for the shock. The men behind it, grinning at the idea of an extra victim, pushed the heavy piano with increased force, only to find that when it hit the Amazon—whom they could not recognize in their present state of impaired memory—it seemed to rebound. Gripping its underside, she heaved mightily and the piano upended. Another shove and it overturned, pinning the screaming men underneath its weight.

With a grim smile the Amazon swung to the two young women, and at the identical moment something hit her across the head with terrific impact. Soundless fire burst and expired before her eyes and then she was looking fixedly at Abna. Behind him were the details of their own bedroom. She was back home again— magically as it seemed.

"Better?" Abna inquired. "I've been using mind-force to patch you up." He eyed her critically. "Yes, you seem to be all right."

The Amazon raised herself on her elbow and looked about her. She was in blouse and skirt—the jacket had gone—and what remained of the garments she was wearing were smothered in dirt and ripped in dozens of places. Even as she became aware of this, she also became aware of something else: her memory had returned.

Every detail was clear in her mind up to the point when she had been hit over the head. She felt her head gently, but so thoroughly had Abna done his healing work and forced physical conditions to obey mental power, the Amazon could feel no trace of injury.

"Good," Anna grinned, holding out his hand and assisting her to rise from the bed. "Vi, you were brought home with a fractured skull and dislocated neck. There were also plenty of deep cuts and severe bruises. It took me about five minutes to put you right.... I hardly need to ask what happened. I was told by the spaceport officials who brought you in that murder had broken loose on the *H-67*."

The Amazon gave him the details and he nodded slowly.

"That's how I pictured it. Anyway, the machine returned safely enough under automatic control, and it was about then that the loss of memory affecting everybody seemed to lift—"

"My special instruments!" the Amazon interrupted

in sudden alarm "What happened to them—?"

"In the lab, waiting for you to sum them up. I had the spaceport executives search your suite, and they found them on the bed. Let's hope they tell us something."

They went to the laboratory and gazed upon the registrations the instruments had made

"Three of these only register normal cosmic radiation," the Amazon said finally, "and it certainly was not that which upset everybody. This fourth one, though, points exactly to the source of the trouble and, by computation, will give us the precise position and distance. I devised it so as to be extra sensitive to any unusual output of power."

With that she began the necessary calculations, using the laboratory's computers to check her results and make sure there were no errors. When, an hour later, she had come to an end of analyzing the detector's findings, her expression was baffled.

"There is something situated about 4,300,000,000 miles away from us," she announced. "Almost in a straight line. In fact, we could fly straight to it by working out in detail the precise source of the power that affected this detector—but as you see, the most amazing feature of all is this mathematical analysis of the radiation that caused the trouble. It isn't physical in the understood sense of the word: it is *metaphysical*."

Abna nodded slowly, musing over the equations, then at last he said: "We're dealing with something decidedly novel here, Vi. As you say, the range is metaphysical, of the same vibration as thought-waves themselves. Some kind of metaphysical radiation was used to affect the minds of those aboard that vessel—and the two vessels before it. I suggest a mass-hypnosis machine being operated from a great distance. Four thousand, three hundred million miles takes us right out beyond Pluto's orbit."

The Amazon pondered. "I don't think mass-hypnosis is the answer, Abna. Hypnotic waves are in the physical order. They are electrical. This is something much more rarefied."

"Whoever is back of it—and one cannot help but suspect Quorne—he surely can't be satisfied with destroying, or otherwise incapacitating, the travelers aboard space machines?"

The Amazon shook her head. "That isn't the ultimate answer by any means, Abna. In the case of the last two assaults, two attributes of mind were temporarily suspended for the passengers. In one case it was scientific knowledge; and in the other it was memory. Something else was undoubtedly blocked in the case of the first crashing space flyer, but we'll never know about that. Using scientific logic, what does that suggest?"

Abna's face had become grim. "It suggests to me one thing only: somebody has tapped the source of all intelligence."

"So I think." The Amazon reflected. "But is that possible? Does such a phenomenon exist?"

"From you, Vi, that's a surprising question! You do not for one moment suppose that your intelligence is your own, do you? It comes from somewhere to begin with, and you express it with results commensurate to your brain power."

"As a scientist I find it hard to acknowledge a fount of all creation, Abna."

"Then take it from me, as a scientist of considerably higher attainments than yourself, that there definitely is a Central Intelligence at the heart of every Universe. It is, as I see it, pure mind-force. Every living being possesses the necessary brain structure to interpret the vast selection of mental gifts being poured out ever-lastingly by this force. It just has to be, Vi. Creation itself couldn't exist otherwise."

They were silent for a moment, looking at each other—and Abna's face was still grim. Then, tapping the bench for emphasis he said:

"If somebody has discovered this force and is able somehow to interrupt its outpourings, almost anything can happen. Yet that, I believe, is what has occurred in these three recent attacks. Mental gifts are not actually gifts: they are certain metaphysical radiations. Block any of them and certain so-called gifts—such as reason, memory, and so on—cease to function."

The Amazon looked at her detector again, then straight at Abna.

"Abna, tell me something. Have you proof that there really is a Central Intelligence?"

"Yes," he answered quietly. "Long ago, when I was the Lord of Jupiter, I discovered such a phenomenon. It actually recorded itself on instruments and was entirely a mental product. I proved it was situated at the exact center of our Universe and radiates its powers outwards—just as normal radio waves radiate from a transmitter. When I discovered this awe-inspiring fact, I ceased to investigate, destroyed all my notes, and dismantled all equipment connected with the experiment."

"But why?" The Amazon looked puzzled.

"For one thing Sefner Quorne was my adviser at that time, and I also knew him to be ambitious. I didn't wish to take any chances of him tapping this metaphysical energy. For my own part I felt I was probing too far in trying to fathom or detect the workings of creation's basis. But now it would appear that somebody has happened on the discovery that I made and is making full use of it. And if it is Quorne...."

Abna left his sentence unfinished.

"He isn't making use of it, Abna. He's *blocking* it somehow—or at least part of its radiations."

Abna turned away from the detector and wandered about the huge laboratory for a space, turning the problem over in his mind. The Amazon, too, became lost in thought. Both of them turned as the warning light on a switchboard advised them that somebody was coming up the driveway. Immediately the Amazon switched in the television screen and studied the visitor approaching the house.

"The minister for the arts!" she exclaimed in surprise, as she recognized the distinguished figure. "A most unusual caller.... You'd better see him, Abna.

I'm not fit to be seen in these rags. I'll change while you deal with him."

CHAPTER ELEVEN
BAIT IS HOOKED

Abna nodded and left the laboratory. Later, when he and. the Amazon saw each other again in the laboratory, the visitor had left.

"Well?" she inquired. "What did he want?"

"He came to tell us that reports have been reaching him from all over the world that musicians, authors, artists, designers, architects, and nearly all other men and women engaged in creative arts have lost their powers. Otherwise they are normal, but their mental gifts have been stolen from them—or so they believe. We are asked to try to discover what has happened."

"You gave him no scientific explanation?"

"It would have been useless. He wouldn't have understood.... It seems evident, Vi, that the metaphysical waves of the Central Intelligence which are responsible for the various creative gifts have been completely blocked. Which seems to suggest it's only a question of time before other intellectual attainments are destroyed also. Incidentally, what does the detector say?"

The Amazon turned to it and released the button.

Then she switched it on again. Immediately the needle jumped and finished up in almost identically the same position as before.

"There we have it," she said. "That same distance of four thousand three hundred million miles.... Abna, if we were to start in the *Ultra II* now, while these mysterious forces are in operation, we'd be guided straight to the source of them as though we had a compass. Save a lot of calculation. This detector will lead the way."

"We'll go immediately," Abna decided.

And within thirty minutes they were on their way, the huge new *Ultra* winging with effortless speed through the deeps. Already Earth was far behind, and the machine was following the course set for it by the unwavering detector.

"'One thing seems obvious," Abna remarked, studying the instrument. "This thing is not so much pointing towards a radiation which is being generated towards Earth, as towards a grouping of power at one particular place. Naturally, if certain metaphysical radiations are being blocked, the instrument will not record something being directed at Earth. What it is actually doing, I think, is indicating a spot where a counter-radiation is intersecting one that ought to be coming towards us."

"Involved," the Amazon commented, "but I gather your meaning. Certainly we are in the midst of the 'blackout,' whatever it may be. I never felt so devoid of ideas in all my life."

"What happens," Abna mused, "if Quorne—and I

am assuming it is he whom we are looking for—gets wind of our approach and turns off, or rather blankets, all the vital radiations like memory and so forth? We'll not be able to stand against anything like that. Certainly repeller shields round the ship won't help us, because we shan't be involved in a radiation but, rather, the absence of it."

The Amazon raised her shoulders negatively. "I just can't imagine what we do in a case like that, Abna. Since we can't think things out clearly, we can only hope for the best."

* * * * * * *

At this time Sefner Quorne was seated in the control chair of his enormous telescope in one of the many observatories of the space-island. Viona, just aroused from a rest period, came into the huge room silently.

"My guess was right, my dear," Quorne said, without raising his head. Evidently he had caught the girl's thoughts.

"Your guess?" she repeated. He motioned to the huge instrument and vacated the observation chair.

"See for yourself."

Viona settled in the chair, and the moment she focused the eyepieces there appeared in the huge circle of the mirror the small speck of the *Ultra II*, growing larger even as she watched it.

"Mother and father!" she exclaimed, looking up quickly; then just as quickly she fought down the joy that surged through her mind in case Quorne was reading her thoughts. Apparently he was not. There was a faraway look in his purple eyes.

"Yes, your mother and father," he agreed. "They have at last decided to investigate the mystery of the Curiosity Tours and the recent happenings on Earth. I've waited a long time for this, Viona, and now I can strike a devastating blow against them."

Viona rose from the instrument, her mouth taut. She was in the difficult position of wishing to appear wholly with Quorne, yet anxious to save her parents from him.

Between the two states of mind, her manner was fidgety and ill-controlled. After a moment or two Quorne noticed the fact and gave his bleak smile.

"Can it be that daughterly devotion is disturbing you?" he asked dryly. "If so, I would remind you that you are the wife of Quorne, and that we have agreed to destroy or incapacitate everything that stands in the way of our final domination of the System and the Universe."

Viona strode forward and caught at Quorne's arm. He revealed no show of emotion as he beheld the obvious entreaty in her eyes.

"Sefner, at least don't kill them! That I couldn't stand, even though I am loyal to you."

Quorne laughed shortly. "I have no intention of killing my bitterest enemies quickly. I prefer to make them dance to my tune for a time before doing that.... Come with me," he broke off curtly and pulled open the observatory door.

Viona followed him into the corridor and then through one of the transparent "spoke" tunnels to the "hub" control room. Here Quorne went immediately to the switchboard of the Dampener and set the controls. Viona watched him helplessly, and after a while he condescended to explain.

"Up to now, Viona, I have dampened the waves which produce the power of creation in the human mind. For that reason, as we know from Earth radio reports, the artists, musicians, inventors, and so forth are bereft of the power to think of anything new. Now I shall go one further and destroy memory and scientific knowledge. Earth people will lose those attributes as well and, inevitably, civilization there will start to go downhill. Your mother and father, being in a direct line between the Dampener and Earth, will be similarly affected. By the time they get here, they will have neither memory nor scientific knowledge."

"Nor will they be able to get here," Viona pointed out. "Remember what happened to the space ship crews; they had no idea how to control their machine."

"I shall not do anything until your parents' machine is near enough to come within range of our attractors, by which means I will simply drag their vessel here."

"And when they arrive, what then?"

"They will be my guests." The idea seemed to be causing Quorne considerable amusement. "With them removed from Earth and Earth's population in the midst of mental chaos, it will not be difficult for me to formulate my plans for taking over control. When I have done that, I will allow Earth people to have their faculties back again, with the warning of what will happen to them if they dare to oppose me. As to your parents, when that time comes...well, we will see. Now go and prepare a meal for me, Viona. By the time I have had it, your parents' machine should be within range."

Without comment Viona turned to go, then a thought seemed to strike her. She looked back at Quorne as he studied the dials of the Dampener.

"Well?" he asked brusquely, as she returned to him.

"How do you propose keeping my parents bereft of their scientific faculties and memory when they are aboard the island here? That will mean affecting us as well, won't it?"

"I am working that out now. I shall assign them to a particular section of the island here and will see to it that a small subsidiary Dampener keeps them constantly in range. I can make the required small extra machine within an hour.... Now, hurry up with that meal!"

Viona left and went into the next department that she and Quorne had taken over as a general living room. In between making the preparations for a meal, she paused as thoughts occurred to her and made notes on a small pad she was carrying in her pocket. There were already about a dozen pages covered with sketches and equations, a complicated formula which Viona was working out on her own account, and every bit of it aimed at overthrowing Quorne. But the time was not yet.

She announced when the meal was ready and Quorne wasted little time eating it. He spoke but little—and then it was usually to complain. When he had finished, he left the room and returned to the telescope. His eyes brightened as he beheld how much larger the onrushing *Ultra II* had become. Quickly he returned to the control room, to find Viona.

"We're ready," he said briefly and snapped the switches on the Dampener. Immediately there was an increase in the humming note the equipment operated.

Moving to the main switchboard Quorne pulled over a switch, studied the instruments, and then nodded to himself. He turned to look at the expressionless girl.

"They are about two million miles distant," he announced, "and the attractors are now drawing them here. In about two hours they will have arrived. Their magnetism will definitely slow down their speed. I have blocked the radiations of science and memory, which effect will also be present on Earth. Later we will learn from radio reports what reaction there has been—granting anybody is able to talk coherently. Two hours gives me just time to build the subsidiary Dampener."

"Do you wish me to help?" Viona inquired.

"I think not. Feeling as you do toward your parents, you might make a deliberate mistake in the wiring so that they could recover their normal faculties. I am ever wary of you, my dear, because I still do not completely trust you.... No, your task will be to watch their approach. Take over the telescope and report to me when they are close, enough to be guided in."

Viona obeyed, leaving the room and heading for the observatory. Quorne gave a grim look after her and then went to work on his subsidiary Dampener. In an hour and a half he had completed his task and then went on a tour of the space-island to decide upon the best quarters for his captives. Eventually he selected the remotest suite of rooms, all of them with walls transparent to the void, and he so arranged the small Dampener and linked it up that the entire area came within its influence. The rest would merely be a matter of using the big machine whilst the Amazon and Abna were brought aboard.

And that time was near. Quorne found Viona looking for him when he returned to the laboratory.

"The *Ultra*'s nearly here," she said quickly. "Another thousand miles and it will crash into us."

CHAPTER TWELVE
PRISONERS OF QUORNE

Quorne nodded and turned to the switchboard. A small viewing screen came to life that gave him a perfect picture of the approaching spaceship. Smiling to himself, he operated the controls of the magnetic attractor, thereby ushering the vessel in gently until at last the gap had narrowed to zero and *Ultra II* was beside the main airlock of the space-island.

"Open the airlock, Viona," Quorne ordered. "Then come back here and stand beside me."

She obeyed, setting in action the electrical controls by which the airlocks were fastened. The moment she had come to Quorne's side, he swung the massive Dampener machine round on its universal bearings and pointed it directly at the inner lock, through which the Amazon and Abna would have to come if they decided to enter the space-island.

After a while the Amazon came into view with Abna behind her. Neither of them were in spacesuits, since the locks of both the space-island and the *Ultra II* were welded together by suction and no air had escaped.

At the sight of her parents Viona started forward,

but Quorne clutched her arm and dragged her back.

"Don't move until you are told to!" he commanded. "You nearly walked into the range of the Dampener!"

She kept her eyes on her mother and father as, having completely entered the control room, they looked about them: Quorne touched a button and the inner airlock closed.

"May we ask where we are?" the Amazon inquired, and though she was looking straight at Quorne, it was obvious she had no remembrance of him. Nor, apparently, of Viona.

Quorne did not answer for a moment. From his fixed stare it was obvious to Viona that he was thought-reading. Finally he seemed satisfied for he relaxed somewhat.

"You are aboard a space-island, my friends, maintained for my own scientific uses. I take it you have no idea how you got here?"

"None," said Abna, his handsome face vaguely bewildered.

Viona looked quickly about her. Her main desire for the moment was to find some heavy object and smash it down on Quorne's head whilst he was thus occupied. Then the mood passed. To do that would certainly incapacitate him and give her parents the upper hand again—but the effect would not be complete. Quorne could not be wiped out by ordinary methods; that had been proven. That demanded a master plan—and part of it was in Viona's pocket, not fully worked out as yet. So, mighty though the effort was, she waited to see what happened next.

"My name is Sefner Quorne," Quorne said calmly. "Might I have the pleasure of knowing yours?"

The Amazon frowned and shook her head. "I cannot recollect my name, nor can my companion. We are suffering from amnesia and have been drifting in space."

"Amnesia in space is not uncommon." Quorne observed dryly. "Oh—forgive me. This is Viona, my wife."

The Amazon and Abna inclined their heads in acknowledgement.

"I must ask you to forgive the gap between us," Quorne continued, still standing well behind the Dampener.

"There are certain electrical radiations here which I require for our sustenance. Scientific, you understand?"

The Amazon and Abna shook their heads and Viona inwardly seethed. To her it was sublime torture to witness her parents, the greatest scientists in the System, so utterly shorn of their power.

"I saw you approaching," Quorne continued, "and so I made provision for you."

"Most kind of you," Abna commented.

"Not at all—purely the hospitality of a spaceman. If you will go down the corridor on your right there to the extreme end, you will find a door. It opens on to your suite. You will find a switch-panel there also. Pressure on the appropriate buttons—all of them are labeled—

will bring you food or whatever you desire.... I would ask," Quorne continued, "that you remain in your suite until your recovery from amnesia. I am engaged in deep experiments and do not wish to be disturbed. You understand?"

"Perfectly." the Amazon responded. "And it is gracious of you to extend such hospitality—"

"Mother!" Viona burst out, unable to contain her emotions any longer. "Don't you and father recognize me?"

Quorne's eyes glinted even though he continued to smile with frozen geniality.

"I'm your daughter!" Viona insisted. "Your daughter Viona! Doesn't that mean anything to you?"

The Amazon gave a puzzled smile. "I am afraid it does not."

"You must forgive my wife." Quorne apologized. "She has been on this space-island so long the radiations are affecting her brain somewhat. Hallucinations are common with her."

The Amazon nodded gravely, then with Abna behind her she went up the corridor Quorne had directed, opened the door at the far end, and vanished within the suite with Abna close behind her.

Quorne watched the distant door close and the swung the Dampener back to its original position, so it pointed directly toward the metaphysical waves affecting Earth—then he looked fixedly at Viona.

He did not attempt to strike her: he knew too well her stupendous strength, but she could feel the force of his mind probing into her thoughts. With everything she possessed, she struggled mentally to protect herself. Let him get one hint of the plan at the back of her mind and he would undoubtedly destroy her.

"That wasn't very clever of you, my dear," be said finally. "For one who is supposed to be loyal to me it was a most revealing outburst."

"'I couldn't help it, Sefner," Viona muttered. "You don't know how it affects me, to see mother and father like that."

"See it does not happen again." Quorne's face was a mask. "I am prepared to make allowances for your youth, but I'll only go so far.... Now, as to your instructions. You are not to enter that corridor there under any circumstances—and just to make sure that you do not...." He reached to the switchboard and closed a contact. Across the center of the corridor a transparent shield dropped rigidly into position.

"That also prevents your parents escaping from their quarters," he explained. "I know you might try and communicate with them, hence my precaution. In their present state they cannot read your mind, and you certainly cannot read theirs. They will stay there until I see fit to release them—nor will they be uncomfortable. Everything needful is in their suite, and with their mentalities impaired as they are, they will never suspect that they are captives."

"I assume," Viona said, with an effort, "that everything in the area of their suite is under the influence of that subsidiary Dampener?"

"It is, and it is well concealed in case you conceive the idea of tampering with it." Quorne reflected and then added, "I would without hesitation bereft you also of your faculties, Viona, if I had the time to build the necessary instrument and the inclination to keep it constantly trained on you. As it happens, I have other things to do—but I shall keep an eye on all your actions and one wrong move will be the finish for you. Understand?"

"You still don't believe I'm loyal to you, do you?"

"I certainly do not—even less so after that outburst to your mother! Now, go to your own quarters and I'll tell you when I want you. I am waiting for reactions from Earth before deciding on how I shall take control. When that happens, I shall call on you for unswerving assistance."

Viona gave him a bitter look, no longer concerned with keeping up the pretence of allegiance, and left the control room.

* * * * * * *

Entering her own room, Viona wandered moodily to the armchair and sat down. For a long time she relaxed, gazing out through the transparent walls on to the abyss of infinity. In one way she was intensely depressed by the circumstances surrounding her: in another she was glad that her parents were aboard the space-island. Even though they were mentally useless, there was moral support in them actually being at hand.

It occurred to Viona after a while that perhaps she

was taking a good deal for granted. Suppose her parents were not really mentally 'shorn' at all, but posing for reasons of their own? There might be a way to find out.

Rising, Viona went to the further transparent wall and gazed through it. From this position she could see the glass-like suite where her parents had been sent, and presently she descried them both, seated in chairs, gazing out on to space. From this position, Quorne in the hub of the huge wheel, could not see what was going on, so Viona wasted no time in fetching her radium torch. Facing it through the wall she flashed it on and off, and at length the intense intermittent brilliance attracted the attention of the Amazon. She said something to Abna and they both came close to the glass-like wall of their suite.

Immediately Viona flashed a message in interplanetary code, known throughout the system: "Are you playing a trick? Do you really know that I am Viona?"

There was an interval then. Evidently not having a torch with them, Abna resorted to using a mirror. The light it caught from the far distant sun was extremely faint, but it was just enough for Viona to detect the signals. And what she read made her heart sink: "We do not understand. Excuse bad signaling. Memory of interplanetary code is only vague."

Abna ceased his effort with the mirror and with a sigh Viona turned away, tossing down her torch. There was no doubt about it now: her parents were not 'putting on an act'—they were genuinely out of commission mentally, unless somehow the Dampener at work on them could be stopped.

Viona considered this as she flung herself in the armchair again. What good would it do to restore her parents? No more good than if she had hit Quorne over the head, as she had almost done earlier. Ascendancy over him would only bring a return of the old battles, and probably his temporary escape and later reappearance. No, the master plan was the thing. There, surely, he would be utterly destroyed forever.

Viona dragged her notes out of her pocket and studied them, then for a long time she went to work with further calculations. It was obvious from her expression that they did not satisfy her, for finally she pushed them irritably in her shirt pocket.

"What's the use?" she sighed. "I'll never work it out without computers and specialized knowledge. And in the meantime, Sefner does just as he likes. Maybe more immediate measures would be best after all."

CHAPTER THIRTEEN
EMOTIONAL OUTBURST

To Viona the line of least resistance now seemed the most attractive. Release her parents! That was the best course, perhaps, and let her grandiose scheme, on which she had labored so fruitlessly at intervals, go overboard for the time being.

Her mind made up, Viona left her room and returned to the control 'hub' where, entering silently, she beheld Quorne seated listening to the radio. Announcements were coming in clearly in the voice of an obviously harassed Earth announcer.

"...that the decline of human intellect seems to have set in. Experts are not yet sure of the cause of the atavism, and indeed they themselves are becoming involved in it. The situation is becoming more chaotic with every hour, nor is it known where Miss Brant and Abna, the heads of the government, have gone to. They promised to aid the artists and other creative people when they were stricken down, but instead of doing so, they vanished from our midst. There is a feeling among the people, stripped as they are of all the veneer of culture, that Miss Brant and Abna have themselves caused this trouble. That they have plotted in the past to bring Earth to subjection is still remembered.... Further news items will be given later."

Quorne switched off and turned to look at Viona as she came toward him.

"I thought," he said, "that I told you I would inform you when I wanted you?"

"You did, but I am unable to rest. And in any case, I don't intend to be treated like a child."

Quorne smiled thinly. "For some things I am glad you came when you did, Viona. You heard the radio messages?"

"I heard them, yes. I cannot understand what you are waiting for. With Earth civilization disintegrating, why do you hesitate over taking control?"

"Because the descent into atavism is not yet complete. In another twenty-four hours the dampening process will have turned Earth people into little better than savages."

"I see." Viona wandered away, apparently thoughtful. Since her back was to Quorne, she was able to study at leisure the switchboard, one of which switches operated the transparent shield across the corridor where lay her parents' suite. In a few moments she noticed it, thrust firmly into place, but she took good care not to betray her discovery either by thought or action.

"You are remarkably restless," Quorne commented, watching her narrowly.

She turned back to him. "How can I help but be, with my parents only a few yards away, and both of them as unknowledgeable as children?"

"You must get used to it," Quorne retorted, getting to his feet.

Viona hesitated, her blue eyes brightening. Then suddenly the force of her emotions got the better of her and she sprang forward. Before Quorne realized what was happening, her fingers had clutched his throat with the tightness of steel springs. He tried unavailingly to drag himself free, but instead was borne to the floor and pinned there, both by the grip on his throat, and Viona's knee on his chest.

"Stop making a fool of yourself!" Quorne panted, struggling savagely. "This sort of thing isn't going to do you any good, Viona!"

She snapped: "I'm going to give you a taste of your own medicine, and give my parents a chance to recover and deal with you."

With that she leaped up suddenly and swung Quorne on to his feet. She forced him by sheer strength toward the giant Dampener that was exercising its influence upon Earth. As he saw what was intended—that he should be thrown into the radius of the machine—Quorne renewed his frantic efforts to break free, but in Viona he was dealing with somebody as strong as the Amazon herself, and his efforts were unavailing.

Only when she came near the switchboard did Viona release her hold on his arm for a moment so that she could snap open the switch operating the shield over the corridor. She saw the shield slide up out of position and at the same time she shouted with all her strength.

"You two in the suite there! Come out here! Quickly!"

Quorne twisted, taking every advantage of the brief seconds in which he was held less securely. He twirled so far around that Viona's hold on his collar was wrenched free. Immediately she hurled herself at him again, but he adroitly twisted and shoved with both his hands as Viona stumbled past him. The result, as he had hoped, was that she lost her balance and went stumbling backwards into the area of the Dampener.

Dazed, she hit the floor with her knees and looked about her. Quorne was standing with his ray gun ready, his eyes glittering. But Viona had not the slightest idea who he was, how she had arrived in her present position, or even her own identity.

"That's the last time you'll try anything like that!" he warned her, and reaching to the switchboard, he flung the shield switch back into place just as the Amazon and Abna, who had heard Viona's voice, came to investigate. The shield stopped them, and since they were still within the area of the subsidiary Dampener, they made no effort to explore further, but simply returned to their suite, talking to each other.

Quorne glanced toward them as they turned away, then back to Viona as she struggled to her feet. She rubbed her forehead dazedly, trying to force remembrance back into her mind.

Quorne motioned his gun and at that she came forward—and out of the range of the Dampener. Then she realized the position in full. But now it was too late to do anything about it with the ray gun turned on her.

"Come with me!" Quorne said.

Viona hesitated, her fists clenched.

She was on the very verge of risking her tremendous strength against Quorne's gun, then prudence stayed her. She went ahead of Quorne down the transparent passages until he directed her into a small room perched out on the end of one of the "spoke" tunnels, its walls, floor, and ceiling of glass. He slammed the door, pushing over the heavy clamps.

Viona looked about her, and everywhere there were stars—overhead, under her feet, to either side, in front and behind.

Quorne returned to the hub control room and then pulled out the shield switch. He swung around the big Dampener so that its influence would radiate over all points in front of him. Then he snapped on a radio speaker connected with the Amazon and Abna's suite.

"My friends, would you be good enough to come to the control room?" he asked

After a brief interval the Amazon and Abna appeared, and as they were held constantly in the range of the Dampener—which took over the influence where the subsidiary one left off—they had no return of their normal faculties.

A few feet away from Quorne, standing behind the instrument, they paused.

"Your stay here need not be indefinitely prolonged," Quorne explained. "Have you any knowledge of the planet Earth?"

"None," the Amazon replied, and Abna shook his

head.

"You will find it quite a pleasant world," Quorne continued. "I have made arrangements with the government there for you to be well received. Certainly you will find it better than staying on this space-island where I am performing very dangerous cosmic experiments which might blow us all up at any moment."

"We could not wish for anything better," Abna said. "On Earth maybe we can find experts who can explain, or even cure, our strange mental trouble."

"Very well, then. There is nothing to stop you leaving immediately. Please forgive me for not coming from behind this machine, but, as I told you, there are certain electrical radiations that I must absorb in order to stay alive. I will open the airlocks for you, my friends."

Quorne operated the necessary switches and then inclined his head gravely as the Amazon and Abna took their departure. Quorne watched their progress intently, presently switching on intervision screens so that he was never for a moment out of touch. Only by this means could he keep the Dampener's radiations constantly affecting them.

So presently they entered the *Ultra II* and the locks closed automatically behind them. Quorne turned to the force-beam apparatus, by which means he would be able to guide the huge space flyer all the way back to Earth. He spent a few moments determining the mathematics involved and then switched on the power. Immediately *Ultra II* began to move.

Viona witnessed the machine's departure with a heavy heart. Whither it was bound she had not the least idea, but with its disappearance went her last hope of being able to obtain her parents' aid in her predicament.

Which automatically brought her mind back to her master plan. She still had her notes with her in her pocket—unknown to Quorne—and also a pencil. So at the final disappearance of the *Ultra II*, she sat on the transparent floor with the void yawning below her and studied her figures by the weak light of the far distant sun. And gradually something occurred to her. At this particular point of the space-island she was able to see every point of infinity and study it at her leisure; something she had not been able—or else had not had the opportunity—to do before. And because of it, certain celestial mechanics she had overlooked began to become apparent.

Lost in thought, she gazed on the inscrutable face of infinity, entirely unaware that the computations and equations that formed gradually in her mind were directly presented by the Central Intelligence itself.

* * * * * * *

For the Amazon and Abna the journey to Earth was just a journey and nothing more. Quorne guided the machine unerringly, as he had promised he would, with the one definite purpose of returning his bitterest enemies to a world populated now by atavized human beings, continuously bereft of the powers of memory, reason, and general conception.

On Earth the effects of the blocked radiations were varied. Here and there the neutralization was not entirely complete, and in these case memory did remain, but all the other attributes which go to make up a law-abiding, sanely balanced human were absent.

In London in particular a few men and women filled this capacity of leadership, an individual by the name of Fletcher Ross being at the head of things. He tried his utmost to bring the demoralized people to their senses—without success, since the basic cause of normalcy was entirely stopped.

To this disastrous state of affairs the Amazon and Abna were returned, their space machine being set down gently at the formerly busy London space-port. Then Quorne withdrew his guiding control and the Amazon and Abna discovered how to open the airlock and then stepped outside into the mid-morning sunlight. Almost immediately they beheld a shouting mob of men and women surging across the enormous area toward them. All of them were disheveled, wild-eyed, and obviously the victims of near-hysteria.

"I wish I could understand all this," the Amazon muttered, pressing finger and thumb to her eyes. "What are we doing here, my friend? Who are we? What is this ghastly dream-sense that has fallen upon us? Can you remember where we have come from? I certainly cannot."

"Nor I," Abna answered, his eyes on the people. "And from the look of things we are not in for a very comfortable time as far as these folks are concerned."

"The Amazon and Abna!" somebody shouted amidst the mob, evidently one whose memory was not entirely gone. "They have had the nerve to come back after all they've done to us—after all they promised. They've come back to gloat over their handiwork!"

The Amazon and Abna, both aware that the rayguns in their belts were intended for some protective purpose or other, pulled them into their hands and leveled them, which had the effect of slowing down the rush of the mob. Puzzled, the Amazon surveyed the vindictive faces.

"Who are you?" she asked.

"Who are we, she says!" somebody yelled. "We're the people you've driven into madness and death!"

CHAPTER FOURTEEN
IN HANDS OF THE PEOPLE

The mob swept forward in such overwhelming numbers that the Amazon and Abna found themselves swamped before they could even fire their weapons. Aided by their stupendous strength, they gave a very good account of themselves before they finally went under. Then the mob fell away from them and they staggered to their feet, cut and bruised, to find about half a dozen armed men and women surrounding them. There was about them a more sane air than was apparent anywhere amongst the rioters.

"You are under arrest," one of the men said, and it was noticeable that he was wearing a queerly designed badge. "My name is Fletcher Ross and, in the present extraordinary circumstances, I am self-appointed dictator."

"Thank you, at least, for saving us from lynching," Abna said.

"Lynching is against the law, but the people have a case against you and, therefore, you will both be tried in a people's court,"

"Case against us?" the Amazon repeated in wonder.

"Why? What have we done? As far as we are aware, we have never set foot on this planet before."

"The bluff is not very convincing, Amazon!" Ross snapped.

"Amazon?" The Amazon looked morel bewildered than ever. "You mean that is my name?"

"Perhaps you prefer Violet Ray Brant?" Ross asked. "Come with us."

They were taken to a large atomicar and whirled through a city which had changed but little—save for the obvious signs of senseless vandalism here and there—but as far as people were concerned, their slinking movements and blank faces were evidence enough of the horror which had stricken them.

Had the Amazon and Abna been at all in possession of their natural senses, they would have recognized the huge edifice at which the atomicar finally drew up. It was the chief government building where the Amazon had her own suite of offices, at the very summit of the 1,000-foot building. Since, however, nothing registered with them, they submitted passively to being led into one of the anterooms. Here they were told to sit down and were given food and drink, and medical attention for their injuries.

Fletcher Ross remained in the room, but he had dismissed his immediate companions. He was a very tall man, stoop-shouldered, with a hatchet-face which bespoke a fair percentage of intelligence and good humor under normal conditions.

When the medical men had departed, he came

forward.

"I have been studying you both," he said, "and I think you really meant it when you say you have no recollection of anything."

"Certainly we mean it," Abna retorted.

"Do you think it would help revive your memories," Ross asked, "if I explained who you are and what the people believe you have done?"

"No harm in trying," the Amazon shrugged.

"Very well, then. You are Violet Ray Brant, better known as the Golden Amazon, and you are the self-styled queen of the Solar System. This man is Abna of Jupiter, your husband, and between you, you rule the destiny of this world and all the others as far as Pluto. Until recently the people revered you both for all you have done for them—then something went wrong. First creative power was lost and you promised to put things right. You departed into space, both of you, and whilst you were away memory and reason slipped from human beings in seventy percent of cases. I, and a few others, managed to retain more or less normal reasoning.... The people believe that with your super-scientific powers you deliberately caused this state of affairs, mainly because there was once a time when you tried to subdue this world by sheer force. That is the situation."

"Which doesn't ring an answering chord anywhere," the Amazon sighed, and Abna also shook his head.

"I am prepared to believe that," Ross said. "I am even prepared to believe that something—some alien power perhaps—is at work in outer space causing all this trouble, and that you have fallen under its influence as has everybody else.... The people rightly demand that you stand trial for what they think is your villainous handiwork, and in the absence of proof that you are not responsible, there can only be one verdict."

"Then let them have their trial," the Amazon said quietly. "There is nothing we can do about it."

Ross pushed a button on the wall.

In response his immediate followers came in.

"Advise the people that a trial will be held," he said curtly. "And see to it that every protection is given to these two prisoners. I shall fill the capacity of judge. Have the courtroom prepared."

* * * * * * *

On the rim of the Solar System Viona was lost in thought, but as little gleams of inspiration came to her she made notes quickly and then sat silent again on the transparent floor, musing over things which were extramundane.... Her speculations were finally interrupted by the sound of the door opening, and Sefner Quorne came in.

He appeared vaguely surprised at beholding the girl squatting on the floor, a stack of notes held in one hand.

"So you decided to occupy the time?" he asked briefly. "Very sensible of you, my dear. I decided to relent and release you—chiefly because I feel lonely myself. There is no reason why from here on you should not behave yourself with your parents out of the way."

Viona hardly seemed to hear him. She was looking at the notes in her hand. Quorne strode over to her.

"What is that you have been doing? Give those notes to me!"

"Certainly not!" Viona looked at him fiercely. "Attempt to take them from me and I'll kill you!"

"Oh, very well. I shan't attempt to upset your childish pastime."

"There's nothing childish about this! It's a formula, or a map if you prefer, for the greatest journey that any scientist could ever hope to make."

Quorne's purple eyes narrowed.

"What are you talking about, girl?"

"I'll explain—if I can have a meal."

"Yes, I'll allow you to now. That is why I came to release you."

Still with her notes in her hand, and the same curious look of abstraction in her eyes, Viona followed Quorne to the hub of the space-island. A meal had been set for both of them, and as Viona sat down at the table she became aware of the radio, tuned into Earth.

"A report on the trial of the Amazon and Abna of Jupiter will be given in detail as soon as available, Fletcher Ross presiding. For the moment, that is all."

"What does that mean?" Viona asked sharply, and Quorne grinned.

"It means, my dear, that I have driven your meddling parents into a most hopeless position. They will be condemned to death, and when they have paid the penalty, I shall step in with my plans."

For some reason Viona smiled and Quorne, after a vain effort to read her thoughts—which he found crammed with equations and speculations upon the infinite—looked at her in curiosity. He simply could not fathom her mood.

"I shan't step out of line again, Sefner," she promised. "We have something much too wonderful to accomplish between us. I have the course of a marvelous journey, but only you have the scientific knowledge to build the machine which can take us."

"Come to the point!" he demanded, as Viona started on her meal.

"Very well." Viona looked at him directly. "Why don't we journey to the Central Intelligence?"

Quorne looked at the girl fixedly.

"How do we know where the Central Intelligence is situated?" he asked.

Viona indicated her notes on the table and Quorne looked at her in amazement.

"But this is impossible!" he exclaimed. "I admit the existence of the Central Intelligence, certainly, but to know its exact situation is something which just cannot be done."

"I have done it," Viona said.

"I would like stronger proof than those sketches and mathematics, Viona."

"I've shown you how you can have it. Construct a machine to follow the course shown in my master sketch there, and then you will have your proof. A space machine like the patched-up *Ultra* should do, but it will require certain alterations in power distribution, because the source of the Central Intelligence is so far away we shall need to travel far in excess of light for very long periods."

Quorne pulled the notes toward him. Viona made no effort to stop him. She went on with her meal and watched him intently at the same time.

"I have tried on several occasions to locate the position of the Central Intelligence," Quorne said presently, without looking up. "How is it that you have succeeded where I could not?"

"Perhaps I spent more time on it: perhaps I have greater powers of inspiration." Vona gave a mysterious smile. "Who knows? Remember that I have unusual parents, Sefner, and from them have inherited many gifts of scientific divination. At first I calculated in the ordinary fashion of cosmic mathematics and made little progress. Then when I was shut in that little transparent room with infinity all around me, the whole pattern dropped into place."

"It did?" Quorne studied her again, wondering, and with her hands she made an all-embracing movement.

"The stars give the answer, Sefner, if you have the scientific insight to interpret them. They fall into an exact mathematical pattern, and they all point to one central position. I became conscious of that when I had infinity all around me. The stars were no longer just constellations and familiar groupings, but cosmic pointers, each one mathematically indicating the way to the basic power, which, in the beginning, created them."

"Then," Quorne said, "your discovery was not so much the work of mathematics as sheer metaphysical inspiration converted into a formula or a plan?"

Viona nodded slowly. "You might call it that. My mother and father both have that gift, but I don't think you have."

"I'm perfectly sure I haven't," Quorne confessed frankly, "and I shall most certainly need very convincing proof before I will admit that you have it, either. These computations seem logical enough, and so does this plan, which guides us straight from here into the precise center of the Universe, located beyond the base of the Milky Way."

"After which we keep on traveling," Viona said. "The center of the Universe lies in depth—absolute depth. As far as I can tell, we can only actually approach the Central Intelligence by moving into the fourth dimension, which is—to put it crudely—the inside of the inside. You understand dimensions, for once you invented equipment which could operate in the fifth and sixth dimensions, so I am sure the fourth should not present any difficulty. It will mean converting the *Ultra* yet again, of course."

"I can do it," Quorne said, pondering. "Make her capable of exceeding light several times, and also make her able to turn aside geometrically from three dimensions into four.... Yes, it can be done." He was silent for a while and then said: "This is a most wonderful thing you have discovered, Viona. As a scientist, I congratulate you. You have actually accomplished something that I, for all my knowledge, do not understand. If you are right, we may be able to absorb unlimited gifts from the fount of all intellect."

"That is my hope."

Quorne resumed his study of her notes and Viona did not interrupt him, but she smiled to herself as she realized that she had explained herself away by the most fantastic nonsense she had ever conceived. Particularly audacious had been her declaration that the stars themselves fell into a certain pattern. Yet in no other way could she satisfy Quorne's curiosity, and most certainly it would never do to state that her inspiration had come directly from the Central Intelligence itself. Once he became aware of that, Quorne would probably become suspicious.

CHAPTER FIFTEEN
TEMPORARY RELIEF

The radio, coming to life again, disturbed the quiet of the control room.

"Stand by for first report on the trial of the People versus the Golden Amazon and Abna of Jupiter.... In the absence of their being able to prove that they have not brought about the sudden atavism upon Earth, they have been sentenced to death."

Viona got to her feet, her face horrified. Quorne grinned complacently and waited for a further announcement. In a moment or two it came.

"The People are against scientific means of terminating the existence of the Amazon and Abna, chiefly because their minds are no longer able to grasp such methods. They have insisted on a way they can understand—primitive, but certain. Therefore, the Golden Amazon and Abna will be burned at the stake in London's Central Square three days from today. That is all."

Quorne switched off and found Viona looking at him fixedly.

"Burned at the stake!" she repeated in horror. "No!

No! They can't do it!"

"They will," Quorne told her. "And nothing you can do will alter it, Viona. I only wish I were present to witness it."

Viona looked about her desperately. All kinds of ideas raced through her mind, from flinging herself on Quorne and choking the life out of him, to seizing the Dampener, near at hand, and switching off its devastating influence. All of which notions Quorne read and pulled his ray gun from its holster.

"I warned you once, Viona," he said, "and I'm doing it again. You and I work alone, and you can forget your parents. In twelve hours I can convert the *Ultra* as required, and then we could make our journey to the Central Intelligence and back. In that time your parents will finally be out of the way, and I can take control."

Viona did not say anything. The ray gun was a powerful deterrent, and she also knew in her heart that only Quorne visiting the Central Intelligence could possibly bring his schemes and his life to an end. Which made it imperative to make the modifications to the *Ultra* as quickly as possible.

"I'll help in whatever way I can," she offered, and Quorne put his gun away.

"Very well. We'll examine the *Ultra* immediately and see what has to be done. Come with me."

Viona rose to her feet, allowing Quorne to go ahead of her to the door. As she left the room in Quorne's wake, she allowed her shoulder to bump against the huge Dampener. Immediately it swung slightly leftward on its universal mounting. Unless examined closely the shift would probably not be noticed—but out in space at the end of the radiation beam the aggregate change in position was tremendous, moving the dampening beam nearly 20,000 miles from its original position and thereby allowing the normal radiations of the Central Intelligence to continue their course, uninterrupted, to Earth.

* * * * * * *

In the heart of London the Amazon and Abna were in their cell in the massive metropolitan jail when they first became aware of a change in their mentalities. At the same time every man, woman, and child in the world became conscious of the ability once more to remember things, to conceive new ideas, to pick up the threads of life where they had been forced to drop them. It was like awakening from a cloudy dream, and inevitably the awakening brought with it heartaches, horrified recriminations, and intense remorse for bestial acts committed.

"Abna, you realize what has happened?" The Amazon was the first to speak.

For some minutes she and Abna had been assimilating the surprising fact that memory was flowing back to them, that scientific knowledge was being restored.

"Yes, I realize what has happened," he answered, the strong sunlight through the window throwing his face into a mask of concentration. "We've come back to normal."

He came over to the Amazon and sat beside her.

"I'm just thinking of the ghastly thing which has happened," she said. "We actually went to a space-island, were introduced to Quorne and Viona, and we did nothing about it! Abna, we've got to get out of here quickly and return to that space-island. Quorne is at the back of all this."

"Obviously," Abna muttered. "And he has Viona in his clutches, too. It seems to me that our original theory of him somehow neutralizing metaphysical waves was exactly true. Now for some reason, he's released us."

The Amazon shook her head. "He'd never do that, Abna. There is some other explanation; perhaps even Viona herself doing something to help us."

Abna snapped his fingers. "That instrument behind which Quorne constantly kept himself was the very one causing such trouble. We've got to get back there as fast as possible."

"Depending," the Amazon said grimly "on how willing the people are to let us go! Don't forget, we have been condemned to death!"

He rose, crossed to the massive steel door, and then gazed at it steadily. Very slowly it began to become transparent and finally vanished entirely.

"Good," Abna grinned. "Evidently I haven't lost the old power of ruling matter with mind. Let's get on our way."

The Amazon beside him, he hurried down the corridor and so into the main hall of the jail. Here there were two armed men standing at attention, and they turned in amazement as they beheld the two prisoners approaching them. Instantly they leveled their weapons.

"You take the right-hand one," Abna murmured. "I'll take the left."

The Amazon nodded and she and Abna continued with their approach at suddenly accelerated speed, watchful for the jet of fire from the guards' weapons. The instant it came they flung themselves forward in a tackle, missed the incinerating beams by a fraction of an inch, and brought the two men to the floor. After which there was only one answer. In a matter of seconds both men were stretched out unconscious from a series of smashing blows.

So the doorway was reached. The Amazon and Abna looked into the street, troubled by the sight of drifting people, not all of them apparently fully recovered yet from their atavism by any means. For which there was a very good reason: they did not possess the highly attuned minds of the Amazon and Abna, and there fore the metamorphosis back to normal was bound to take longer. Memory had definitely come back, but the deeper brute instincts had not yet been supplanted by normal reasoning and culture.

Accordingly, as the Amazon and Abna decided to make a dash for it to the spaceport where they remembered they had left *Ultra II*, they found themselves pursued by an ever-increasing mob of people—and by the time they were halfway to their destination it became impossible to proceed any farther.

"Have you fools no sense?" the Amazon demanded. "You are surely aware that the trouble under which you have been laboring has lifted?

"Partly," answered a man in the forefront. "But how do we know it isn't some kind of a trick on your part, Amazon? Or yours, Abna?'

"Talk sense!" Abna snapped. We were in jail up to a short time ago. What chance could we have there to do anything?"

"There's such a thing as remote control, and both of you are experts at it as you've proved in the past," a man said. "You're heading for the spaceport to make another getaway into space. But you're both under sentence of death, and that sentence is going to be carried out!"

The man strode forward determinedly and caught at the Amazon's arm.

Instantly she snatched it away and lashed out with her left fist. The man never saw it coming, and he dropped senseless.

"Any more?" the Amazon demanded, whipping out the gun taken from a guard. "If you people won't learn sense by the ordinary way you'll have to have it smashed into you! All of the things that have happened to you have been caused by Sefner Quorne, and those of you whose memory has returned cannot fail to remember him!"

"Quorne?" repeated a woman in the front. "You mean he's caused our losing a grip on things?"

"He has! And he did his best to subject Abna and me as well. For some reason his influence over us has stopped for a while—and that is why it is essential that Abna and I move quickly. We know where Quorne is—out beyond Pluto where he has built a space-island, from which he is operating the apparatus which has held all of us in thrall up to now."

"For your own sakes you have got to let us through!" Abna insisted.

He looked over them swiftly and then threw his tremendous mind-force. Dealing with so many individual wills at once was a major task, but at last he obtained a result as somebody shouted:

"Let them through! They must be speaking the truth because they couldn't do anything in jail. If it's Quorne back of this, anything's better than having to fight him!"

That was enough. The people began to fall away and give free passage. The Amazon re-holstered her gun and looked about her.

"You won't regret this," she promised. "It's a wise decision, and the one you should have made at first."

With that she followed Abna's hurrying figure down the wide street, and the men and women followed on their heels, apparently intent now on seeing that nobody else tried to interfere.

Nor did they. There were few people at the space-port, and they had no chance to do anything. At last the Amazon entered *Ultra II* with Abna close behind her. He closed the airlock and gave a sigh of relief.

CHAPTER SIXTEEN
NEARING THEIR GOAL

The changes in the *Ultra* were complete, and Quorne said: "Just a final check over here and then we can start our journey."

Viona's eyes wandered to the slightly deflected Dampener. "But surely, Sefner, there is nothing to check? We can leave the repelling shields around the island while we are gone to keep away anybody who might investigate—a most unlikely happening."

But he started to check everything.

"How has this happened?" he demanded suddenly.

"What?" Viona turned. "Oh, the Dampener. What about it?"

Quorne's purple eyes bored at her for a moment, then he made an examination of the readings on the universal mountings. Very carefully he shifted the apparatus around somewhat. This done, he looked at the girl again.

"Have you been tampering with this?" he demanded.

"When would I have had the chance to do that? I've been with you all the time!"

"That's true," he admitted, frowning. "Yet somehow

this Dampener had been moved. It cannot be locked in place, unfortunately, since it relies on float-balances. As the island moves at times due to distant planetary gravitations, the Dampener has to correct itself on the balances. No matter: it is tuned back into position now and should be safe enough until we return."

They entered the *Ultra* and the journey began.

"Let me see," Quorne mused, studying the master sketch Viona had worked out. "We follow an exact straight course for the Milky Way moving at full velocity—which, with the power plant converted as it is, means several multiples of the speed of light."

"Correct," Viona confirmed, for despite her inner worries concerning her parents, she was nonetheless profoundly interested.

"You contend," Quorne asked, as he began to build up speed steadily, "that the Central Intelligence is situated there?"

"Toward the base of the Galaxy," corrected Viona. "In the direction of Sagittarius."

Quorne nodded.

And while this amazing journey was being pursued, other events in space were also being enacted in the region of Mars. For, within the *Ultra II*, the Amazon and Abna had just become aware of the slow evaporation of their knowledge of science and powers of memory.

"Put in the automatic control!" Abna cried as the Amazon gave him an anxious look. "Maybe it will save us. Quorne has blocked the radiations again."

The Amazon reached to the appropriate switch that activated the automatic controls, which no radiation blockage could affect. And even as she relaxed again, the old look of dumb vagueness came over the Amazon's face and she pressed finger and thumb to her eyes. Abna gave her a glance, his own tremendous mind surviving longer than hers. He turned to the window and saw ahead of him the giant outer planets with Pluto in the far distance.

"We dare not risk going on," he said quickly. "Jupiter's field is likely to drag us down. Safest course is to turn back."

The Amazon looked at him vacantly, slumped helplessly in the control chair. Abna leaped across the control room and disengaged the switch for remote control, then with the last remnants of memory he had left he turned the *Ultra II* about in a. gigantic circle and set the course for Earth.

In this he made a cardinal blunder, the outcome of his muddled thinking. Earth was certainly straight ahead but there was a much more powerful attraction which would make itself felt before Earth could be reached, and that was the pull of the sun itself, the Earth being situated on its other side, as it pursued its own orbit around its primary. Vaguely, with his last vanishing threads of memory, Abna comprehended his mistake, but he could not think fast enough to rectify it.

The Amazon got slowly to her feet and moved to his side as he stood gazing through the enormous observation window.

"What is wrong?" the Amazon asked hesitantly, noticing Abna's taut expression.

"Everything. We should have gone on, Vi. You were right. It seems to me that the sun—" He stopped, unable to figure out the problem any further, and certainly the Amazon could not.

So, for a time at least, *Ultra II* followed the Earthward course which Abna had set for it, but inevitably the master field of the sun began presently to make itself felt as the machine came closer to it. Ordinarily, at this point, the *Ultra*'s drift would have been checked by recoiling the vessel away from the intruding field, but, as things were, no such precaution could be taken. At last she was pointing straight at the flamboyant day star. This, at least, put an end to the Amazon and Abna's gazing. The blaze of the sun was too intense for them to even glance at it; so they turned away into the control room and looked at each other worriedly. Fortunately, the abeyance of memory also made them more or less unable to realize how deadly was their danger. Nothing could save their ship from plunging into the sun.

* * * * * * *

Meanwhile, Viona and Quorne were still being transported at constant, terrific velocity across the wastes of infinity. The acceleration having reached maximum, velocity was constant and, therefore the weight that had existed had now ceased. The strain on heart and lungs had lifted to feather lightness, and Viona slowly began to recover consciousness and looked about her. Quorne, too, was showing signs of life, color returning to his cheeks.

Viona waited for a few moments, absorbing the situation, and then she eased herself from the pressure couch and moved to the switchboard, adjusting the neutralizers so that they produced an Earth-norm gravitation. This done, she looked through the observation window upon a scene that she had already viewed in the prismatic mirrors.

The First Galaxy was greatly nearer, but even yet many light-centuries had to be traversed. Quorne got up, too, and his first move was to check their speed.

"Eminently satisfactory," he muttered. "Believe it or not, Viona, we are already traveling at 90% of the speed of light itself."

"I can believe it," Viona answered. "Yet how obvious it is now that speed and distance is relative. We have no sensation of movement. It seems as though the Universe is whirling past and we are standing still."

"The lack of—or, rather, absence of—acceleration is conducive to that effect," Quorne replied, and went over to inspect the power plant. He found everything in order and put in another copper bar for when it should be needed. Then he again consulted the chart that Viona had drawn up, checking the course by instruments.

"Everything satisfactory," he announced. "We are so far away from the Earth System we could only find it by mathematics and, of course, everything is dark out there."

He turned to look at the abysmal interstellar void outside the hurtling space-flyer. Before the vague terror of the view could overwhelm him, Quorne turned back to Viona.

"Prepare a meal," he ordered. "I'll check on the Galaxy. We have to know the exact point at which to move into the fourth dimension."

"I can tell you from memory," she replied. "At our approach to the fifth celestial quadrant, which has Sagittarius as its center, we make our transference into four dimensions, by which we fly into depth within depth at infinite velocity relative to the normal three-dimensional universe."

With that she turned away to begin the prosaic task of preparing a meal. Quorne looked after her, vaguely puzzled by her uncanny celestial knowledge; then when he came to check up the equations for himself and verified them on the computers, he found that she was exactly right.

Distance was devoured as the time passed by, and the immeasurable vastness of the Milky Way grew upon them. Now they were coming closer to it, they could discern for the first time the exact nature of this sprawling, misty island of light. It was not entirely composed, as most astronomers had believed, of countless millions of stars—so close together they appeared to form a continuous sea of light when viewed at vast distance—but of pure misty light, suggestive of that of a nebula. Yet even this did not quite fit the picture.

There was a gossamer quality about the Milky Way, in the midst of which the genuine stars like Antares and Epsilon glinted with all the cold brilliance of real matter, whilst behind them stretched the everlasting curtain of soft, embracing light.

"There's a heavenly quality about that light," Viona muttered, gazing at it through the window. "Did you ever see anything so pearly, so all-embracing, so gentle?"

"I am a scientist, Viona, not an idealist," Quorne replied curtly: "No scientist of true vintage refers to a celestial phenomenon as being heavenly. That amounts to paganism."

Viona did not make any further comments since, obviously, they would be quite lost on the atheistic Quorne. He, for his part, sat appraising the Galaxy while he finished his meal, then he crossed to the switch-board and spent some considerable time studying the instruments.

"We are 3,000,000 miles from the fifth celestial quadrant," he commented at length, "which means we must start slowing down our velocity in readiness to swing into the fourth dimension at the exact point in space we've calculated."

Viona nodded. Sagittarius, the center of the fifth celestial quadrant—a measure of space used by space pilots—was apparently growing now with every second that the *Ultra* devoured the distance. Everything in readiness, his hands on the controls, Quorne watched the star intently and also the compass and directional pointers which kept the vessel straight in line—then at length he restarted the power plant in reverse and immediately the headlong flight began to slow down.

Even so, the *Ultra* was still moving at stupendous velocity, and Quorne had all his work cut out to exactly determine the moment when he must make the switch-over from normal space to four dimensions. Viona came to his side and checked the instrument readings by her own equations—then at length she raised her hand.

"Now!" she exclaimed, under the impulse of a great inner prompting.

Quorne did not question her accuracy; he plunged in the switches and, as far as the vessel was concerned, nothing seemed to happen. There was no lurch, no check to the speed—but outside everything had changed incredibly. The Milky Way had completely vanished. Space was entirely empty without a single star or nebula.

Quorne's face was troubled as he peered into the ghastly dark.

"Now where are we?" he asked, glancing up at Viona: "Not a thing to be seen! Are you sure your mathematics were correct?"

"Perfectly sure. You checked them, didn't you?"

"As near as possible, yes—but surely there ought to be signs of something?"

"Why?" Vlona asked quietly. "Surely you know that light is a material manifestation? It doesn't belong to the metaphysical range. The metaphysicals are always invisible."

"Meaning," Quorne asked slowly, "that the true fourth dimension is entirely metaphysical?"

"At this point in the universe it seems to be, yes. We cannot see anything because our eyes are not attuned to metaphysical radiations."

Quorne looked at the instruments. Then he got to his feet and crossed to the special panel on the far wall.

"These can show us what our eyes cannot see," he said. "If there is anything metaphysical here, it will be distinctly visible."

He moved the switches and almost immediately the various detector screens began to flash with livid, unexplained energies, proving beyond doubt the presence of tremendous metaphysical radiations outside the vessel.

"According to the scale reading," Quorne said, "we are in an enormous sea of radiation which can variously be classified as memory, reason, creative intelligence itself—in fact, the very same radiations which, in a weaker form, I blocked in normal space. I confess don't understand the situation at all."

"Well, I do," Viona said. "Normally, viewed through material eyes, the fourth dimension is just a blank, but actually, when you have the instruments to prove the fact, it is seen to be filled with the invisible radiations of mental power, all of which emanate from the Central Intelligence. There is a theory widely held among scientists, dating as far back as the twentieth century, to the effect that once upon a time everybody thought, acted, and saw four-dimensionally until the concept of it became so clouded over it was lost to sight. If it is ever referred to at all, it is called sixth sense—"

"Yes, yes, I know all about that," Quorne said impatiently. "To what are you leading?"

"To the fact that the Central Intelligence of the Universe is four-dimensional and the material creations are three-dimensional, which is why no living being has ever looked upon the Central Intelligence. Maybe there were some who did in the remote Biblical times; but that is not our concern in this super-modern scientific age." Viona moved closer. "We, Sefner, are also human beings, matter creations without the necessary physical mechanism to see the Central Intelligence face to face, but we have the instruments which can see him—or her, or it. One cannot apply a sex to the mind of the universe, I suppose.

"You said," Quorne remarked, "that when we came near enough to the Central Intelligence, we would absorb all its secrets and turn them to our own account."

"I still say it," Viona answered. "How can we help but do so? If one approaches close to a fire, one cannot help absorbing its heat. For the first time in history the Central Intelligence cannot remain hidden by reason of being four-dimensional because our instruments can bridge the gap."

Quorne said: "We have only devised such instruments by the medium of intelligence, which must have been derived from the Central Intelligence itself in the first place. Why should it be willing to impart the knowledge which enables us to see it when mysticism and secrecy is its chief objective?"

"I can't answer that," Viona shrugged. "Switch on the main screen and see if there is anything in view."

Quorne closed the requisite switches, and immediately, upon the largest screen, there appeared a single, brilliant star of indeterminate size and very far away.

Quorne looked at it and his expression of wonder deepened.

"In the fourth dimension a star should not look like a star," he commented.

"We have no evidence that it is a star, as such," Viona replied. "In fact, I'd say it is highly unlikely. There would be other stars to keep it company and maintain the general balance."

"I never before beheld an object which can't be measured or computed," Quorne said. "It doesn't make sense!"

"It does if it is not material," Viona answered. "There are no instruments for measuring the depth or distance of mind, or the center of metaphysical radiation. Sefner, I believe that object is our goal—the Central Intelligence itself!"

* * * * * * *

Midway between orbits of Mercury and Venus and traveling sunward at a prodigious pace, the *Ultra II* was continuing its drift toward the major gravity. The Amazon and Abna were gazing vacantly before them. Then by imperceptible degrees their consciousness, memory, and reason once more asserted themselves.

Ultra II was moving at three-quarters the speed of light towards the sun, and was 40,000,000 miles from him. A considerable distance, but so terrific was the solar attraction there was great doubt as to whether the *Ultra* could be slowed up and reversed rapidly enough to escape destruction.

Suddenly there had come a report like a gun, and a thin acrid, smoke drifted from the switchboard.

"Too much load! The circuit-breaker's out of action." The Amazon gave an anxious glance. "We're just racing our power plant to bits against this field—"

"We're losing ground," Abna said. "Only on half power by the look of things. We need something which can carry the load for brief intervals and then drop it now and again—"

The Amazon got to her feet quickly, her face grim. "Take over the controls, Abna. I'm going to try something for myself."

CHAPTER SEVENTEEN
STRANDED IN SPACE

"What have you in mind, Vi?" Abna asked, settling in the chair. The Amazon didn't answer, and Abna twisted to see what she was doing. Suddenly he guessed her intention and gave a yell.

"Hey, wait a minute! You're not turning yourself into a fuse, surely?"

"I am. It's the only way we can get the make-and-break effect we want. I understand the load of this power plant better than you do, otherwise you could try it. Here I go!"

With her right hand the Amazon seized the opposite pole of the fuse switch and immediately her lithe, powerful body became rigid as the current surged through it. Her lips taut, she held her ground, though her feet were visibly quivering on the metal floor.

"Give—give it everything you've got," she whispered, her face glistening.

Abna did as he was told, and with a massive surge of energy he threw the reversal power straight towards the dragging field of the sun.

The retarding effect on the hurtling *Ultra II* was

immediately evident, and the Amazon held on as long as she could with her gigantic resistance. Then for a second or two she relaxed and gave the power plant, and herself, a chance to recover.

The process was repeated—and again, and at each effort the speed of the *Ultra II* became slower and slower.

"Now!" the Amazon panted, nearly at the limit of her strength. "Everything you've got to pull away from the sun!"

Abna snapped the switches, his gaze jumping across the instruments, then to where the Amazon was hanging on desperately, her trembling feet braced on the metal floor. Just how much current she was absorbing and 'earthing' she did not know, but there was definitely a limit to what she could stand.

Suddenly she gave a little cry and sagged backwards, sparks flying from her hands as they were torn by her weight from the switch. Abna slammed in the robot control and stumbled to take her place.

He held on with everything he possessed, his limbs a seething torment of cramp as the current tore and twisted through every nerve. Dazedly he watched the velocity reading. It was advancing more quickly now—and quicker still. The battle was slowly being won. He relaxed for a few seconds, then came back to the terrible task, and held on to it, save for brief pauses, until the *Ultra II* had gained sufficient momentum to pull free of the counter attraction.

Only then did he release his hold, and cut the power

plant down by half. He replaced the burnt-out wiring on the switchboard. There were anguishing seconds for him as he watched if momentum, on a reduced scale, was maintained. It was. The *Ultra II* had definitely pulled clear of the danger area.

Abna swept up the Amazon's limp form in his arm and laid her on the wall couch. A restorative injection brought her round after a few moments, and she looked about her. Her inner chagrin at having lost consciousness was not improved in any way by the sight of Abna's cheerful grin.

"Nothing to worry about," he said. "We've pulled clear! You took too much on yourself with that load. It nearly finished me, let alone you!"

"I can take anything you can!" she retorted, sitting up.

"But you didn't, Vi. You went out cold—and I don't blame you. Convinces me you're not so superhuman as you think under extreme conditions."

She got to her feet and snapped back the shield from the windows. A brief glance at the sun and a check on their speed assured her that everything was at last under control. Turning to the switch panel, she swung the vessel's nose until she had she had a set course for the not-far-distant Venus.

"Venus should be well out of the 'neutralized' area being produced by Quorne," she explained.

"And when we get to Venus, what de we do?"

"Rest with the colonists, take on a fresh supply of power bars, and then set off to deal with Quorne. I propose to attack him by his back door."

Abna frowned. "Back door to what?"

The Amazon said: "We know that Quorne has contrived some kind of space-island, out beyond Pluto, and it is from there that the trouble is coming. If we attacked from the front we would, as you say, find ourselves in the same predicament as before. So instead we go round the back—taking an enormous detour through space and avoiding the neutralization that is being directed at Earth. From the fact that he stood behind one of his major instruments when we saw him, I remain convinced that to rearward the neutralization had no effect."

"But he'll see us approaching and immediately start to 'amnesify' us."

"I'm going to take a chance on that," the Amazon replied. "We'll approach the island to rearward at high speed—and we'll keep up that high speed until we ram him! His island may be big, but it can only be braced by force beams, and an armored cruiser like this *Ultra* ramming into it will not only inflict a terrific amount of damage, but will also swing the neutralizer beam off target and, let us hope, will send the whole island crashing towards Pluto, the next nearest field of attraction."

"And Viona?" Abna asked quietly.

A struggle passed over the Amazon's perfect features. "The destruction of Quorne's apparatus is the main thing, Abna—and his death too, if it can be achieved without him recreating himself somehow.

Viona will have to be sacrificed."

* * * * * *

In the depths of four-dimensional space Quorne and Viona looked for perhaps the sixth time at the solitary point of light towards which their machine was hurtling, still at an almost inconceivable velocity—yet even so the pinpoint did not appear to have grown any larger.

"I begin to think it's an illusion," Quorne said irritably. "And I also think we're wasting time! I reckoned three normal days and nights for our round trip and considerably more than that must have elapsed. I am in favor of starting back home."

"How?" Viona asked calmly.

Quorne gazed at her. She was seated in the comfortable chair before the main observation window, gazing at the utter dark outside. Only on the screen was the solitary star of the fourth dimension visible.

"How?" Quorne repeated. "By turning back, of course!"

Viona laughed softly. "You can't turn back now, Sefner. The instruments don't direct the way through four-dimensioned space. You might go round in a circle forever and. never discover how to get out."

Quorne's mouth set harshly and he turned to the switchboard, but the more he tested the various controls and studied the instruments, the more he realized that Viona had spoken the truth.

He said: "Did you realize when you suggested this

preposterous trip that we could never get back?"

"I knew it was a possibility."

"Then how did you hope to absorb the secrets of the Central Intelligence and turn them to account if we're to stop in this alien space forever?"

"You can't see the answer to that?" Viona asked in surprise. "Really, Sefner, you astonish me!"

He made an angry stride towards where she was seated, then he pulled up short before the unexpected sight of a slim ray-pistol in her right hand.

"Better not," she cautioned, all her levity gone and a cold glint in her sapphire eyes. "I've worked hard for this, Sefner, and I don't want to spoil everything by turning into a murderess—so keep your distance."

Quorne turned away again, fighting down his fury.

"Worked hard for this?" he repeated. "What do you mean?"

"I'm interested in only one thing, Sefner—your total destruction, physically and mentally."

"For my wife you show great consideration," he observed, with all his old poisonous politeness.

"I'm your wife only because you hypnotized me into going through the ceremony, and where we are now those vows are meaningless. I'm your bitterest enemy, Sefner—perhaps even more so than my mother and father, because all the time you have used me as a tool. You've taken constant advantage of my immaturity, as you call it. For that reason, a resounding victory over you will be all the more pleasurable."

Quorne shrugged. "You have your victory now, my

dear, so why make a song about it? We're lost and never shall we get back home. What more do you want?"

"Your elimination!" Viona's lips tightened. "That has yet to come...," and her eyes strayed to the growing star on the screen.

Quorne's expression clearly showed that he was baffled, and he certainly could not read anything from the girl's thoughts: she kept them constantly jumbled. But deep down he was still afraid—not of the immediate predicament of being stranded in an unknown and unknowable space, but of Viona's curious complacency, and the vague suggestion that she knew something he did not. It frightened him and exasperated him by turns.

"You are an atheist, Sefner, are you not?" she asked after a while, toying with her gun gently.

"All true scientists are!" he retorted.

"Not necessarily. I am not, and I—"

"You are not a true scientist! You're a young woman with a lot of amazing ideas and no true gift of detached analysis."

"I got us this far, anyhow!"

"Which proves my point, otherwise you'd have worked out how to get us back!"

"You read the equations. As a true scientist you should also be able to find the way back.... As a matter of fact, I do know how I shall get back, but that does not include you.... However, we're wandering from the point. You are an atheist, which means you do not admit the presence of an all-directing power behind the Universe."

Quorne smiled cynically. "I have never said that. As a scientist I am prepared to admit a directive intelligence—and indeed we are proving that one does exist. So what is your point?"

"Just this. You have the consummate audacity to think that you, one scientific man in the midst of infinity, can actually take secrets from the Central Intelligence and use them! Of all the colossal conceit! And it is the very thing that is going to destroy you, Sefner. I've based my calculations on your overfed ego from the very start!"

"Can it be," Quorne asked, "that you are actually veering on the side of religion? That doesn't mix, Viona! As you well know, science and religion have been antagonistic for centuries."

"Everyone is entitled to worship whom and what he pleases—but I am—and always have been—willing to acknowledge that no power of human devising could possibly hold together the Universe, mental or physical. Others admit it too when they realize their own shortcomings. Even my mother, one of the most dominant scientific women who ever walked the Earth, admits at times that only a super power can account for some of the miracles which do happen. The theologian would call this super power God, and so does the average man, woman, and child. A scientist—Sir James Jeans of the twentieth century—called this super power the Supreme Mathematician, because he believed the whole Universe to be a mathematical conception. Others refer variously to the Grand Designer, the Absolute Artisan, and so forth. Everywhere there is this acknowledgment of a power outside ourselves.

"You call it the Central Intelligence because, as a scientist, you have gone far enough to prove its emanation of mental powers which we utilize. Were you content with that discovery? Were you content to acknowledge this controlling power? No! You considered yourself clever enough to interfere with it! You blocked the radiations it emanates for the benefit of living beings. You did something I tremble to think of—defied the Central Intelligence itself!"

Quorne smiled coldly. "In a universe ruled these days by power-science, and wielded by such people as your parents and myself, it becomes perfectly permissible to bend even the source of all intelligence to one's own ends!'"

"And you dare to think you can get away with that?"

"I have already done so!"

"Have you? You are lost in this region, which belongs entirely to the Central Intelligence. How do you imagine you are going to escape?"

There was silence. Quorne turned away and resumed his study of the screen. The solitary star was now growing bigger, and with this increase there came an almost intolerable amplification in the amount of light it was emanating. Quorne turned away, rubbing his smarting eyes, and then considered.

"Unusual for a star to give forth such intense light at such a distance," he commented.

"The answer being that it is not light as such," Viona replied.

CHAPTER EIGHTEEN
MISSION ACCOMPLISHED

Quorne blazed at her: "We'll get out of this space before we're finished! And with every secret we want as well!"

Viona made no response. She sat looking at the screen, until it dawned upon Quorne that she was apparently suffering no hurtful reaction. He moved over to her.

"It doesn't hurt your eyes?" he questioned.

"No, I wouldn't be such a fool as to sit here gazing if it did."

Quorne sat down nearby, clenching his fists. At intervals he darted glances at the screen, felt an unknowable something bite into him and then looked away again. Finally he returned his attention to the girl.

"Maybe I have assumed too much," he said slowly. "I haven't put any limits on the power I can attain."

"No doubt of that," Viona agreed callously.

"Listen to me, Viona. I am prepared to admit that I went too far in believing I could go one better than the Central Intelligence itself. I am even prepared to renounce the idea of trying to absorb its secrets. You say you know how to get back. All right, let us return and forget this fantastic adventure. We've attempted too much."

"We can't turn back now, Sefner."

"But you said—"

"I said that I know how *I* shall get back. I do—but not yet. We are both controlled by that Central Intelligence. You came here because I was ordered to bring you. My only reason for knowing that I shall safely return home afterwards is because I know I have done nothing wrong. I have merely discharged a duty."

"You mean to tell me that the planning of this journey, every detail of it, was put into your mind?"

"Every bit of it. No scientist in the normal way— not even my mother and father—could possibly have worked out such intricacies by mere individual effort."

Quorne smiled crookedly. "In fact, a plan of vengeance against me, aided and abetted by Central Intelligence?"

"In the first place, there was the desire for revenge, yes—the wish to get you into an inextricable situation. Afterwards it took concrete form as ideas and formulae poured into my mind from an unknown source. You are here because the Central Intelligence wills it. I am merely the instrument who made it physically possible."

Quorne turned away in contempt and for a moment or two stood beside the table, beating his fist gently upon it; then at length he seemed to arrive at a decision.

"Very well. Now we know the situation! I shall make use of it and the Central Intelligence can do its worst! We'll come out of this alive, Viona, and when we have done so, I'll deal with you. You'll never try and drag me into a trap again."

"There will be no necessity," Viona replied.

Quorne gave her an angry glance, but his temper did not prompt him to physical violence. Viona's ray-gun was too handy, for one thing, and her strength was too tremendous, for another. So instead, Quorne pulled up the second chair, placed it before the screen, and looked at the growing star.

The onwardly speeding *Ultra* seemed at last to come within measurable distance of the star. Sheer fascination forced Quorne to stare at it, but as he did so, trying his best to ignore the anguish he was enduring, he realized more than ever that here was no star in the accepted sense. It was a globe of some kind, but apparently composed entirely of violently pulsing light. Or was it light at all? Quorne was becoming convinced that what his human eyes saw as light were actually metaphysical radiations, the very essence of all thought-bases, and the closer the approach to the Central Intelligence, the more impossible it became to look at it.

Quorne closed his eyes, but that did not stop the growing flood of intangible waves of thought which had started to engulf him. His brain was becoming a turmoil. He was an idiot and a genius at one and the same time. He knew all things and yet he knew nothing.

He had all power and yet was impotent to use it. It even occurred to him once that the Central Intelligence was deliberately playing with him, giving him supernal gifts and then snatching them away from him.

This very fact enraged him. Never in his life had he been treated in this fashion, and such was his opinion of his own scientific powers he opened his eyes abruptly and glared in fury at the four-dimensional screen.

What happened then Viona did not know; for her back was turned, but she heard Quorne give the most unearthly groan, as though every vestige of reason were being drained from him. She resisted the temptation to turn and see what was happening. Had she succumbed to it she would have seen Quorne's face had become blank, imbecilic, and that the stare he was directing at the screen was sightless and dead.

He lurched a little and put a trembling hand on the switchboard. His voice came, low and gasping:

"Viona! Help me! Help me!"

Viona remained motionless as long as she could, then at last curiosity was too much for. She jumped to her feet and turned, just in time to see Quorne becoming slowly transparent as he sank helplessly to the floor. In a matter of ten seconds he had dissolved completely, and not a trace remained except the flying kit he had been wearing.

Viona kept her face averted and groped her way to the four-dimensional switches, snapping off the screen that had contained the baleful 'star'. With it extinguished, as far as being visible was concerned, she felt better able to look about her.

There was no doubt about it. Quorne had utterly vanished and, despite the bitter feelings she had toward him, there settled on Viona a deep overriding fear at finding she was alone. Her hand moved back to the switch and almost touched it in readiness to bring the Central Intelligence back onto the screen, then an inner sense—if such it was—made her hesitate. So far she had not looked at the fount of all intelligence, so why do so now?

"Home!" she whispered. "I must get back home."

She inspected the instrument readings, but they were still at zero. There was no indication how fast she was being carried along—no indication of anything, indeed, except the slow awareness of ideas, even of a voice, which could have been her own speaking in her consciousness.

"You have been wise so far: continue to be so. Move the seventh switch in the first row on the main control panel."

Mechanically she did so.

"Now the fifth switch in the third row...."

Again she obeyed.

"And the eleventh switch in the first row."

Viona completed the instructions without having the least idea why she did so. Nor was she sure whether the voice she could hear was her own vivid imagination, sharpened by the extraordinary conditions, or whether it was pure thought emanated from somewhere outside the vessel and presumably from the

Central Intelligence.

"You completed your mission, Viona of Earth, and brought to me Quorne of Jupiter. For that, even as you have believed all along, no harm shall befall you—as you will presently see. Quorne dared to emulate my powers. He believed he could take my place and decide what is right for the Universe—hence my instruction mentally that you bring him to me. You need have no fear. He will never return. You have the answer to your problem concerning your return home. I have named the switches that can transport your vessel back to your normal space and time. Once you are there, I shall remove from your mind all memory of how to return here."

Viona waited, her eyes closed, convinced that the mental messages had not yet finished.

"I am the Central Intelligence," came the vibrations again. "And though I represent the basic unit of thought for the entire Earth universe, from which all thinking creatures derive their intelligence, I am not the Ultimate of Ultimates, whom some of you designate as Almighty. Where that power lies none can ever know. It is the pure metaphysical outpouring from which such as I—a mental unit—am created.

"For every universe there is a unit such as I, and there are universes without number within each other and without each other, all of them embedded in a Supreme One whom none can understand or fathom. Suffice it then, Viona of Earth. You have not communicated with Supremacy, only with an unswervingly obedient servant thereof. As I am obedient to the power that created me, so you have been obedient to me, who provides your thought forces, your reason, your every mental attribute. Go then—and never return!"

Motivated by something other than her own will Viona snapped over the subsidiary power-switch, used as a rule in an emergency only. Her action threw her to the floor, so violently did the *Ultra* lurch. As she lay there, wondering vaguely what new manifestation of the Central Intelligence was going to take place, she realized that all sense of being overwhelmingly dominated had gone and that she was watching a vivid circle of light on the metal floor.

Sunlight! Or was it perhaps from Sagittarius? She got to her feet quickly and stumbled to the window, heaving a great sigh of thankfulness. She was back in normal space with the *Ultra* traveling swiftly, unguided at the moment, in the vicinity of the Milky Way. The light was pouring in from the great ocean of the Galaxy itself.

Shaken by her experience, but still filled with a vast relief, she looked at the switchboard and beheld the instruments functioning as of yore. The curious combination of the switches she had moved, each one fitted .to the four-dimensional control board, had instantaneously projected the *Ultra* clean out of the fourth dimension into ordinary space, and to Viona there remained not a clue as to how to ever enter it again if she had wanted....

She reversed the three switches to their neutral positions and then with the astro-compass set the course for the distant system where lay Earth and home.

CHAPTER NINETEEN
TIMELY APPEARANCE

Following a few hours' stay at the Venusian colony under its protective dome, the Amazon and Abna wasted no further time in getting on their way, hurtling the *Ultra II* in a tremendous detour through the System so that they finally emerged some 20,000,00 miles to the 'rear' of Pluto—or, more exactly, 20,000,000 miles farther into the Greater Deeps than Pluto's orbit.

At this point the Amazon slowed the great vessel down and began a meticulous search of the void through the high-power telescope—but though Pluto himself showed up clearly enough, there was no trace of the space-island.

"Hardly to be expected at this distance," Abna said.

"Then what are we to do? We have to know the exact position in order to set the course and then get up enough speed to ram the island out of existence."

Abna reflected. "Since we are at the rearward of its neutralizing radiations we'll certainly not get any reaction on our instruments which might reveal the position—and we'll never see it until we're right on top of it because, as we know, it is transparent. The only thing to do is use the simplest method of all—long-distance radar—and see if we get an 'echo.' Then we can fix our position exactly."

"Using radar occurred to me long ago, Abna, but the trouble is it will reveal itself on Quorne's instruments and he'll fling everything he's got straight at us."

"He'll do that anyway when he sees us hurtling toward him. Better risk it."

The Amazon hesitated, then at last she switched on the radar equipment and adjusted the controls, 'feeling' her way in the void for 20,000,000 miles ahead. One reaction came very rapidly until it was obvious it was a reflection back from Pluto—so the searching began again until at length there came the second 'throwback,' and the cascade of sparks across the screen which revealed the presence of an object some 2,000,000 miles from Pluto itself and to one side of it.

"That's probably it," Abna said finally. "No means of being sure. We'll have to chance it. Set your course. We'll know fast enough whether we're right or not as we come to the end of our run."

Her yellow face carved in troubled lines, the Amazon worked out the details of the course and then set about making the giant spaceship conform to it. Abna watched in silence, a frown deepening upon his forehead.

"Why do you keep hesitating, Vi? You're not feeling your memory slipping again, are you?"

"Nothing like that, Abna. I'm just thinking of Viona.

Up to now I have been perfectly satisfied in thinking that we cannot discriminate, but now it actually comes to it, I—well, it isn't easy. Yet we can't warn her. If only we could somehow detach her from Quorne."

Abna shook his head gravely. "There's no way, Vi. All you can do is go straight ahead."

So, reluctantly, she put her hands on the switches and started up the power plant. Then she settled herself firmly in the control-chair and kept her attention fixed on the view ahead—at present one of empty space, except for the nearest planets themselves. Their speed gradually increased and Abna, conscious of the tremendous shock that would come when the space-island was struck, settled down in the second control-chair and watched intently through the port.

Faster the *Ultra II* traveled, and still faster, achieving at length a speed of half that of light At this tremendous velocity the Amazon kept the rate constant: it was more than sufficient within the confines of a System if total destruction of the *Ultra II* were not to ensue.

The 20,000,000 miles dwindled rapidly at the terrific pace the machine was moving and the radar screen showed clearly that the still invisible object ahead was sweeping ever nearer.

"Strange Quorne doesn't throw everything at us," Abna commented. "He must surely be aware of our radar beam and there is no reason why he can't spot us now, telescopically."

"May be his rest period," the Amazon answered. "I surely hope so. It may give Viona to chance to get free—"

"There it is!" Abna cried suddenly, bracing himself.

The Amazon gave a taut nod. Out of the blackness the great mass of the space-island had at last become visible as a wheel, its outer rim and hub distinctly traced out in thin lines, but the spoke-tunnels were still invisible. So much the Amazon and Abna had time to observe—then so stupendous was their power dive the island seemed to flash up to meet them, devouring the void as they hurtled on with undiminished velocity.

The shock when the *Ultra II* struck the island was stupendous, and the Amazon had definitely under-rated the strength of the bracing ray that held the island steady. In consequence, although the *Ultra II* smashed clean through the hub of the island and sent the whole amazing structure hurtling in the direction of Pluto, the vessel itself took a tremendous hammering. It seemed to bounce backwards on the initial shock, then it flew through the midst of flying masses of transparent material. Its speed was, of course, tremendously checked, and in the doing a white-hot heat was generated in the prow by the conversion of the collision into energy.

Half senseless in their seats through the impact, it was a few seconds before the Amazon and Abna realized they had not achieved the armor-plated victory for which they had hoped, for though they had smashed the island to pieces, the *Ultra II* was fast losing air as the momentarily superheated outer plates fissured and cracked like glass before a raging fire as white heat met interstellar vacuum.

"Spacesuits!" the Amazon gasped, striving to keep her senses as she felt the air draining away from her. "Get them, Abna. I can't make it."

Abna himself, too dazed to get control of the situation through mind force, dragged himself out of his chair and gulped desperately for breath. The last traces of air in the control room revived him momentarily, and he reeled over to the compartment where the suits were kept, but by the time he had it unlocked his senses were fast reeling and he half tumbled to the floor.

The Amazon, very little better as far as breathing was concerned, and feeling also the heat radiating from her body, fought desperately to get to her feet. This much she managed. Then she leaned forward and turned the air pressure screw to maximum. Though the precious vapor escaped as fast as it was ejected, it did for a second or two revive her as she held her mouth and nose close to it. Taking a deep breath and holding it, she staggered drunkenly across the control room, tripped over Abna's body, and then set about opening the spacesuit compartment. But here she was beaten, the loss of warmth from her body had made her hands lifeless and she could not move the already frost-encrusted catches.

Her face purpling slowly, she sank to her knees and her breath escaped in one tremendous surge. Then came the real anguish, when there was no more air left to breathe. Only the vacuum— Her senses blacked out and she tumbled over on her face amidst a conviction of overpowering pressures.

When she found herself awakening again, the incidents that had led up to her unconsciousness quickly returned to her. This, then, must be death. Neither she nor Abna had had any possible chance of escaping from the trap. And yet....

Very slowly she opened her eyes and, to her astonishment, saw the curved metal roof of the control room ceiling. Somehow, though, it appeared different. There were four more stanchions than was usual, and the radio apparatus was in a corner, instead of overhead.

The Amazon sat up with a jerk, and the springs of the pressure couch eased up gently beneath her movements. Her amazement was complete when she found herself looking into the blue eyes of Viona as she sat on a chair nearby.

"Better?" Viona asked and, reaching to the air control, she turned down the pressure knob.

"But how—where did you come from?" the Amazon demanded, her strength rapidly returning. "Where is your father?"

"There!" Viona nodded to the second pressure couch. "He'll be fit to kick himself when he learns he took longer to recover than you!"

The Amazon struggled to her feet, overcame the brief dizziness that sought to overwhelm her, and then crossed to Viona's side.

"You haven't answered my question. Viona! How do you come to be here? And—" the Amazon glanced about her—"how did you patch up those broken plates so quickly?"

"I didn't patch up anything. This is the original *Ultra*, upon which Sefner made repairs while it was in that other space. Your own vessel was drifting rapidly toward Pluto when I came across it, and you and father here laid out cold in the shattered nose. I got you out quickly, brought you here, removed the spacesuits in which I'd fixed you and gave you all the oxygen I dared.... Ah! Dad seems to be coming round."

Ahna raised his great body and surveyed the scene and the two women, then after an obvious struggle to piece things together he hauled himself from the pressure-couch and came across the control room.

"How you come to be here, Viona, I don't know," he confessed, putting his great arm about her shoulders. "Your mother and I were both convinced that you were on the space-island, and when we rammed it we knew it would probably kill you as well."

"Never discriminate, do you?" the girl asked dryly. "Either of you.... It's all perfectly simple to explain. You rammed an empty space-island—smashed it to pieces, incidentally, and you can see the remains on Pluto any time you wish—and but for my happening to be returning to it at the time you did your power dive, you'd both be dead by now."

"Returning to it?" the Amazon repeated. "Where have you been? Where's Quorne?"

"Dead. Completely and finally dead. I have the assurance of the Central Intelligence upon that."

The Amazon and Abna looked at each other blankly and Viona gave a laugh.

"You know," she remarked, "this is a terrible comedown for the two super-beings who believe they can do everything! The little daughter flies in from infinity and saves them from death, and also—entirely on her own, or, at least, obeying the directions of the Central Intelligence—she disposed of Quorne. What you both could not do with all the science at your command, I accomplished single-handed! Now laugh that one off!"

"The very last thing I would wish to do," Abna answered seriously. "The best thing we can do is to have a meal and a rest, during which you can tell us everything."

Viona nodded promptly and set about the task of preparing a meal for the three of them. While she was about it, the Amazon and Abna strolled to the great observation window and surveyed space. They were already leaving Pluto behind—upon which, presumably, there lay the shattered remains of Quorne's space-island and the wreck of *Ultra II*—and were heading toward the orbit of Neptune.

"If the youngster is speaking the truth, it is going to be most humiliating for us," Abna murmured, standing with his hands locked behind him and his gaze directed toward Neptune.

"Why shouldn't it be the truth? She certainly saved us, and Quorne is definitely nowhere to be seen!"

"But she speaks of obeying the directions of the Central Intelligence itself! How in cosmos could she? We never managed to get *en rapport* with the Intelligence at any time."

"I do believe," the Amazon muttered, "that for once in your life you are annoyed, Abna!"

"Not annoyed—just embarrassed. For Viona to be able to do something which we cannot—or didn't—is breathtaking, to say the least."

"When you two have finished your secret conference, the meal's ready," Viona announced, already seated at her place at the table. "Don't worry about the ship; it's on automatic control and the course will take us straight home."

"Thanks for telling us," Abna said huffily. "We are still both capable of reading a switchboard, my dear!"

Viona smiled. "Have some restorative, Dad, then maybe you'll feel better-tempered!"

CHAPTER TWENTY
FOR SAKE OF HUMANITY

Abna and the Amazon sat down and both their gazes converged on Viona. She went on eating unconcerned.

"Well?" Abna asked finally. "What is your story?"

"It's a long one, Dad—better eat while I tell you. You, too, Mother."

Viona told her story in absolute detail. By the time she had finished, the orbit of Neptune had been reached and the *Ultra* was sailing on serenely towards Earth.

"Do you half begin to realize what you have accomplished, Viona?" the Amazon asked finally.

"I know exactly what I've done. I've disposed of Sefner Quorne, the biggest menace to the peace of the Universe who ever existed, even if he was my husband."

"I am not referring to that," the Amazon said. "Though I. admit you have succeeded where your father and I failed. Since you actually saw Quorne vanish into nothing—which means his body and his mind must have been completely dissolved—and afterward received the assurance of the Intelligence itself that Quorne would never return, we may take that as a fact, and thank the cosmos for it. But the point that utterly astounds me is that you went to the source of all intelligence! Whatever put such an idea into your head?"

"The Intelligence itself, I suppose," Viona shrugged a little. "All I know is that when Sefner started talking about a Central Intelligence, and of how he meant to turn it to his own account, it occurred to me that he was overstepping the laws of creation. I reasoned that if the Intelligence knew this, Sefner would be completely eliminated from the scheme of things. However, my efforts to find where the Central Intelligence was situated failed because it—the Intelligence—cannot be traced by normal mathematics. I managed the whole thing by inspirations and ideas received direct from the Intelligence, which shows that he knew all about Sefner's depredations, and made me the instrument by which to bring him to justice."

"Obviously," Abna said. "But the fact remains, Viona, that you are a human being and not a metaphysical radiation There must have been some deep human conviction within you that your effort would succeed, otherwise you would never have had the courage to attempt it."

Viona smiled brightly. "'Do you agree," she asked slowly, "that some of the ancients actually contacted the Central Intelligence?"

"No doubt of it," the Amazon replied. "That is explained by early civilizations possessing metaphysical powers which largely died out with evolution. What remains of it today we call the sixth sense, or psychic gift. Why do you ask?"

"It occurred to me," Viona said, "that the Ancients, making their recording about the Central Intelligence, had said that none could look upon this Intelligence and live. It says that in the Bible, doesn't it?"

"True," the Amazon assented. "But that refers to the Supreme Being Himself and—"

"The Central Intelligence is not the Supreme Being," Viona insisted. "He told me as much. He is only one unit, the unit of intellect back of this particular Universe of ours. Naturally the Ancients would ascribe all power to him, not knowing, as we do, that he represents only an infinitesimal part of the whole mass of mental creation that makes up microcosms and macrocosms.... However, be that as it may, I kept on thinking about that statement—'None shall look upon me, and live.'

"I knew Sefner's insatiable curiosity and terrific conceit, and I reasoned that if we could get measurably near to the Central Intelligence, he would definitely look at it. He most certainly did! Even from a distance it started to wrench his mind, whereas on me it had no effect. I think I know why. I had only obeyed its orders. Sefner, on the other hand, was defying it. Finally, he looked upon it so long he was destroyed, utterly and completely."

There was silence for a while and the Amazon reflected.

"It means, then, that you based your whole astounding escapade on that one statement by a long-dead Testament writer?"

"Why not? The Testament writers told the truth insofar as they understood it. Why shouldn't I believe it?"

Abna said: "And you say this Central Intelligence looked like a star?"

"According to the four-dimensional instruments, yes."

"And when you were close up to it, what did you see?"

"Nothing. I didn't look at it."

"You made that tremendous journey and saw only what looked to be a remote star on a four-dimensional screen?" Ahna was incredulous. "My dear girl, didn't you for one moment realize what a colossal scientific—"

"I realized only one thing—that if I looked upon it I might die, as Sefner did. So I never looked. I felt mind impressions. I knew I was in a sea of mental waves, and I was guided back home. That's all I know."

"The greatest of all scientific achievements thrown away," Abna sighed. "And probably no way to rectify the mistake."

"None," Viona agreed simply. "The memory of how to return to the Central Intelligence was blotted out of my mind. There is no way back. I am quite prepared to accept the fact."

The Amazon said: "Viona did rightly, Abna. I can understand that you with your immense scientific mind would like to try to gaze upon the source of your intellect, but some things are better left unexplored. Sefner Quorne allowed his scientific ambition to override him, but where did it get him when he conceived the idea of being smarter than the power that made him? No—there are enough things in the material world yet to he tackled without plunging into the metaphysical realms.... As for you, Viona, you have done a wonderful thing. You have, as you say, gone one better than your father or I."

"Perhaps because I am both of you and a bit of myself," Viona smiled. "The combination of all three is a mighty powerful product...." Her smile faded slowly and she became thoughtful. "With Sefner gone, the struggle to keep the Universe free of his depredations is over, isn't it?" she asked.

"Presumably," the Amazon agreed.

"Which will make things seem awfully quiet," Abna commented.

"That's what I was thinking—and I have a notion which may save us all from dying of monotony."

The Amazon and Abna looked at her and waited, but she did not immediately explain herself. Rising, she wandered to the observation window and stood considering for a moment or two. Finally she said:

"Sefner had an idea about forming what he called the Universal Brotherhood, by which he meant to carry his dominance to the farthest stars. I am wondering if there isn't a variant on that idea...."

"Such as?" the Amazon questioned, and Viona wandered pensively back to the table.

"We three here represent the most scientific brains in the System, don't we? That isn't egotism: it's a generally admitted fact. And I think it can be truthfully said that we have brought great benefits to all the planets we have taken under our aegis."

"Correct," the Amazon agreed promptly.

"Since we do not foresee any danger to the System in the future—barring the unexpected, of course—why don't we borrow Sefner's great idea, but instead turn ourselves into the Cosmic Crusaders?"

"The *what*?" Abna asked in surprise, and then he grinned. "Sorry, my dear. I'd forgotten you're still only young in outlook."

"Will you please stop referring to my youth?" Viona complained. "I've proved my worthiness to take my place with you by having disposed of the biggest menace of all. And what is wrong with us being crusaders? The dictionary refers to a crusade as being an enterprise conducted in an enthusiastic spirit. And that is just what I am proposing! For too long circumstance has forced us to use scientific power for hostile reasons. We have had to be more concerned with the power to destroy than with the power to create. Perhaps our chance has come at last to reverse that."

The Amazon and Abna waited with tolerant smiles.

"I got this notion when I was way out in the Milky Way," Viona continued, her eyes bright. "It occurred to me then, looking on those spawning myriads of worlds, that it is ridiculous for them all to be detached from each other.... Think what we could make of it if we could unify every planet in the Universe!"

"A tall order," Abna observed gravely.

"Maybe it is, but we can make a start on it, can't we? We have the one thing that surely must be known in greater or less degree by the inhabitants of all the worlds—science. To worlds that have no space travel, we can bring that amenity and so link up the backward planets with the advanced ones. A mighty interplanetary 'know-your-neighbor' campaign. See what I mean?"

"It is possible," the Amazon mused, "that you have a very good idea there, Viona. I have often conjectured myself on the kind of inhabitants some worlds must possess, and how interesting it would be to communicate with them."

"Then let us do it!" Viona spread her hands. "The Earth System is content, and it can soon rebuild the troublesome mess which Sefner caused. Once that is straight, we have the great ocean of infinity in which to travel, crusading with science, helping the backward, contacting the lonely worlds, uplifting the inhabitants of those planets who are at the end of their civilization."

"Again I must remark that your youth ignores the possibility of hostile spirits," Abna remarked.

"What if there are?" Viona gave her sunny smile. "I believe that in the wastes of space, in the tens of millions of inhabited worlds that must exist, we shall in the main find decency and the will to co-operate, because at root every thinking being has more good than bad in his makeup. In the end, maybe millions of years in the future, perhaps, it will be admitted that the Cosmic Crusaders were the instrument by which Universal peace was ushered in...."

Abna picked up the bottle of restorative solemnly and poured out three drinks. He raised his own glass and the Amazon and Viona did likewise.

"A toast," Abna said looking through the great window on to the wastes of space. "To the 'Cosmic Crusaders.' May the missions they hope to make bring to those distant island spaces the benefits and the happiness of the one bond which can make all men and women, no matter of what world or time, eternally united. The bond of science!"

The three glasses rose, and the blazing sunlight through the window reflected back from the sparkling amber liquid.

ABOUT THE AUTHOR

British writer JOHN RUSSELL FEARN was born near Manchester, England, in 1908. As a child he devoured the science fiction of Wells and Verne, and was a voracious reader of the Boys' Story Papers. He was also fascinated by the cinema, and first broke into print in 1931 with a series of articles in *Film Weekly*.

He then quickly sold his first novel, *The Intelligence Gigantic*, to the American magazine, *Amazing Stories*. Over the next fifteen years, writing under several pseudonyms, Fearn became one of the most prolific contributors to all of the leading US science fiction pulps, including such legendary publications as *Astounding Stories*, *Startling Stories*, *Thrilling Wonder Stories*, and *Weird Tales*.

During the late 1940s he diversified into writing novels for the UK market, and also created his famous superwoman character, The Golden Amazon, for the prestigious Canadian magazine, the Toronto *Star Weekly*. In the early 1950s in the UK, his fifty-two novels as "Vargo Statten" were bestsellers, most notably his novelization of the film, *Creature from the Black Lagoon*.

Apart from science fiction, he had equal success with westerns, romances, and detective fiction, writing an amazing total of 180 novels—most of them in a period of just ten years—before his early death in 1960. His work has been translated into nine languages, and continues to be reprinted and read worldwide.

www.ingramcontent.com/pod-product-compliance
Lightning Source LLC
Chambersburg PA
CBHW050730250626
47155CB00005B/1739